advance praise for
& THIS IS HOW TO STAY ALIVE

"A beautiful and rending look at family, loss, and grief, all while sharply dissecting time travel tropes and delivering a powerful message about memory, storytelling, and responsibility. It's a story that hurts in the best of ways, confronting death and healing without losing its sense of humor or its impulse for rebellion."
—Charles Payseur, author of *The Burning Day and Other Stories*

"*& This is How to Stay Alive* is a powerful manual for recovering from grief, exploring intergenerational trauma, and traveling through time. Kagunda's prose is intense and relatable; you'll feel like you're jumping through time with these characters. The perfect read for anyone and everyone."
—Eboni Dunbar, author of *Stone and Steel*

"Highly inventive and brilliantly crafted. Kagunda pushes the envelope in this exceptional novella, playing with time and form as she explores grief and the drama of the human condition."
—Tendai Huchu, author of *The Hairdresser of Harare*

Expanded from the 2020 short story
originally published in *Fantasy Magazine*
and subsequently selected for inclusion in
Best African Speculative Fiction
Best American Sci-fi and Fantasy
Year's Best Dark Fantasy and Horror

Neon Hemlock Press
www.neonhemlock.com
@neonhemlock

And This is How to Stay Alive
Shingai Njeri Kagunda

Cover Illustration by Ejiwa Ebenebe
Cover Design by dave ring

Paperback ISBN-13: 978-1-952086-33-5
Ebook ISBN-13: 978-1-952086-34-2

Shingai Njeri Kagunda
AND THIS IS HOW TO STAY ALIVE

Neon Hemlock Press

THE 2021 NEON HEMLOCK NOVELLA SERIES

NEON HEMLOCK

&
This
is How
to Stay
Alive

BY SHINGAI NJERI KAGUNDA

To the Loveships that have carried me to this point

ONE

BARAKA

The hospital walls are stark white. Pictures hang on one wall, taken over sixty years ago, before our country's independence. White missionary nurses smiling into the lens, carrying little black children, some with their ribs sticking out. This is what fascinates Kabi—she cannot stop staring at the black and white photos. The doctor comes to the waiting room area and Kabi looks away; she knows it in her spirit—she cannot feel me.

It is not until my mother begins to wail that the absence beats the breath out of her. She feels dizzy. The ground comes up to meet her and Dad is holding Mum so he does not catch Kabi in time. The doctor keeps saying, "I am sorry. I am sorry. I am so sorry."

For Kabi, the sounds fade but just before they do, somewhere in her subconscious she thinks she will find me in the darkness.

Yes, she is coming to look for me.

NYOKABI

Funerals are for the living, not the dead. Grief captures lovers and beloved in waves; constricting lungs, restricting airflow, and then when and only when it is willing to go does it go. I try to hold back tears—to be

responsible

oldest

daughter.

Visitors stream in and out. I serve them tea, microwave the samosas and mandazis that aunty made, then transition into polite hostess.

Yes, God's timing is best.

No, as you can imagine we are not okay but we will be.

Yes, we are so grateful you have come to show your support.

No, mum is not able to come downstairs. She is feeling a bit low but I am sure she will be fine.

Yes, I will make sure to feed her the bone marrow soup. I know it is good for strength.

No, we have not lost faith.

But sometimes, sometimes I am in the middle of a handshake, or a hug, or a sentence, when grief takes me captive.

It is a thing that closes my throat, this heavy grief, taking my breath so quickly that I wonder, if only for a moment, whether I am also dying.

TIME

Some stories begin at the end is what I would say if I believed in beginnings and endings.

Some stories are part of every other story, but only part, and therefore cannot speak for every other story. Remember Nyokabi learning to carry stories when she was six? The first time she visited her mum's shags an old man told her a story.

Guka scared her at first. He was so different, so icky, and he smelled kidogo. But just started speaking to her. Kabi pretended not to listen but he told her about the magic plants in the forest that healed the wounded fighters when the wazungu were attacking them. Nyokabi tried not to listen to the old man but she kept thinking about the forest and imagining what it would look like with the green green trees and the red and purple flowers. If she thought hard enough she could carry it in her mind.

I wish you could see her then, falling in love with the kind of words that painted pictures for the first time. When they took Guka back to Nairobi, Nyokabi did not mind as much. In class three, she won the award for the best short story composition and she didn't mind as much when Guka—who still smelled kind of funny—kissed her on the cheek, gave her a little kasuku notebook, and whispered, "You are Njeri returned to us."

She didn't really understand then but she just chalked it up to what Mama had referred to as *his dementia*.

Remember Baraka listening to Nyokabi when he was four?
She would practice the stories on him. He was enthralled. I wish
you could see him then before death was more than a possibility.
Remember how they played in stories of the past when Nyokabi
was eleven and Baraka was nine? It was Guka's funeral, back on
the land where she had heard her first story of the forest. The
funeral was soo so long and all of it was in Kikuyu. Baraka got
antsy. Mama Kabi gave her daughter a look. "Can you keep that
brother of yours quiet?"

If Mama got angry they would both be pinched. "Let's go
play," Kabi whispered, and when the adults weren't paying
attention, they slipped out of the open service and ran into the
tall brick house where Guka and Cucu had lived a lot of their
lives.

"*Pew pew*! Guns of the wazungu!"

In the play version, little Baraka Kimani, still alive, lay on the
ground with a fake wound on his side, pretend dying. Nyokabi
jumped from the red sofa set to the carpeted floor lined with fake
blood made from tomato sauce, giggling. "I am from the future
and I am here to save you!"

Remember that one moment, before the inhibitions of
growing up, Kabi closed her eyes and imagined Guka alive still?
Remember how Baraka said "Of course Guka is still alive!"
Because at nine, to die only meant to go away for a bit, because
at nine, one could not fathom forever.

Remember, between then and now, how many things
have changed and how many things have stayed the same?
Remember then and now.

NYOKABI

"Wasted tears." The lady, one of mum's cousins—second? Or third?—clicks and shakes her head. How long has she been standing there?

I open my mouth, shut. Open again, silence.; I can only lick my wounds and move away. There is nothing to say after that dismissal. I shift, angling my body away from her, lifting my half open silver notebook off the bathroom counter. The bathroom door, slightly ajar, is calling me to the space between its bark and the wall. I will not beg for sympathy. The pen drops and I swear I see a spark as it hits the ground. Can you see sound?

"Shit." The word slips out before I realize who I am in the room with. I pick up the pen and attempt to squeeze past her body which is covering the space I saw as my escape route.

A sucking in of teeth. "Kabi wait!"

I turn my head slightly back; she asks, "What does gone mean for you?"

I am confused by the question; have no time for old woman foolishery, already there is Tata Ciru shouting my name in the kitchen. "Yes?" I answer, because I must be

Responsible

Oldest

Daughter

Always in that order. No time for my tears, no time for

mama's cousin to dismiss my grief. The first *yes* was not heard so I shout again, pitching my voice to traverse rooms. "Yes, Tata?"

And the response: "Chai inaisha, kuna maziwa mahali?"

How to leave politely, because respect; I mumble under my breath something about going to make tea for the guests.

"You have not answered my question."

I sigh, in a hurry to leave, "What was the question?"

"*Gone*, child—these terms that talk circles around death: gone, no longer with us, passed away, passed on—what do you think they mean?"

"NYOKABI?" Tata Ciru is sounding irritated now.

"COMING!" I scream back, and to the woman in front of me, "Gone is…not here."

"Aha, you see but not here does not mean not anywhere."

This woman is talking madness now. I mumble, "Nimeitwa na Tata Ciru, I have to attend to the guests now."

She smiles. "I know you are trying to dismiss me, kairetu, but here, take this."

She slips a little bottle into my hand just as I open the door to leave. "It's a little remedy for sleep, there are dark circles around your eyes."

I slip the bottle into the pocket of my skirt and run to the kitchen, no time to look or to ask, no time to wonder or to wander, no time to be anywhere or to be anything but the

Responsible

  Oldest… only?

    Daughter.

BARAKA

This is how to not think about dying when you are alive: look at colours, every colour, attach them to memory. The sky in July is blue into grey like the Bahari on certain days. Remember the time the whole family took a trip to Mombasa and Kabi and you swam in the ocean until even the waves were tired. Kabi insisted that you could not go to Mombasa and not eat authentic coast-erean food, so even though everyone else was lazy and dad had paid for full-board at White Sands Hotel, the whole family packed themselves into his blue Toyota and drove to the closest, tiny, dusty Swahili restaurant they could find. It smelt like incense, Viazi Karai, and Biriyani. Are these the smells of authentic coast-erean food?

This is how to not think about dying when you are alive: take note of smell, like the first time you burned your skin. The charring flesh did not feel like death. It reminded you of mum's burnt pilau; attach feeling to memory.

"Tutafanya nini na mtoto yako?" Dad never shouted, but he didn't need to.

Mum was chopping vegetables for kachumbari. "What do you mean? Did I make him by myself? He is your son as well."

"Yes, but you allowed him to be too soft."

Her hand, still holding the knife, stopped mid-air, its descent interrupted. She turned to face him, her eyes watery and red from the sting of the onions. "Too soft? Ken? Too soft? Did you see him? Have you seen your son? The fight he was involved in today...he can barely see through one eye. How is that softness?"

Baba looked away, Mum's loudness overcompensating for his soft spoken articulation. "Lakini Mama Kabi, why was he wearing that thing to school?"

She dropped the knife. "Have you asked him? When was the last time you even talked to him, Ken? Ehe?"

Quick breaths. "We went to the church meeting for fathers and sons. I spend time with him."

"Ken, you talk to everyone else about him, and you talk *at* him but you never talk to him. Maybe if you were here more..."

"Don't tell me what I do and do not do in my own house, Mama Nyokabi! Do I not take care of the needs of this house? Nani analipa school fees hapa? You will not make so it looks like I do not take my responsibilities seriously. If there is a problem with that boy it is not because of me!"

Smoke started rising from the sufuria. You reacted, pushing yourself from behind the door, forgetting you were not supposed to be in such close vicinity to this conversation. "Mum, chakula chinaungua!"

She rushed to the stove, turned off the gas, and then realized you were in the room, looked down, ashamed that they were caught gossiping. The smell of burnt pilau.

This is how to not think of dying when you are alive. Move your body; like the first time you punched Ian in the face.

Whoosh!

Fist moving in slow motion, blood rushing through your veins, knuckles-connecting-to-jaw-line, adrenaline taking over: alive, alive, alive, alive, alive. This is how to be alive. This is how to not think about dying when you are alive.

Of course this was right after Ian had called you shoga for wearing eyeliner to school and then said, "Ama huelewi? Do you want me to say it in English so you understand F-A—"

"Go fuck yourself!" you screamed and punched simultaneously.

And of course this singular punch was right before Ian punched you back and did not stop punching you back over and over and over but God knows you kicked and you moved, and you were alive.

NYOKABI

On the night before the funeral, I am exhausted but I cannot sleep. There is shouting upstairs. Mum and dad discussing the service for the millionth time. I close my eyes as if that will block my ears from hearing the sound. A door is banged. Footsteps shuffle down the stairway.

I should go and check if everything is okay but I do not want to. I cover my head with my pillow and count one to ten times a hundred but I still cannot sleep.

I switch on my phone: so many missed calls, and *are you okay?* texts. I see past them, my mind stuck on a thought. Could I have known?

GOOGLE
How to know when someone is suicidal

Offered list by WebMD:
- Excessive sadness or moodiness
- Hopelessness
- Sleep problems
- Withdrawal

The list goes on. All things I have now, things everyone has at some point.

I can hear them whispering in the hallway. The main lights are off so they do not know I am in his room. Mum has been looking for every opportunity to pick a fight with anyone and everyone since Baraka...

I switch on the bedside lamp, look around the room, and feel the need to clean, to purge, to burn—everything reminds me of him. I notice the skirt I left on the dark brown carpet, tufts fraying in the corner of the fabric, a bottle peeking out—bluish with dark liquid and I remember the old lady; mum's cousin, twice removed, or thrice? What have I to lose? I pick at the skirt, unfolding its fabric until I get to the bottle stuck in the pocket. It is a strange little thing, heavier than it should be. I try to decipher the inscrutable handwriting on the white label. One teaspoon? I think it says, but I can't be too sure. I open the lid, sniff it, and wrinkle my nose. The scent is thick, bitter; touching the sense that is in between taste and smell.

I am so very exhausted and I do not want to wake up tomorrow. Can I skip time?   I throw my head back, taking down a gulp. It's thick like honey but it burns like pili-pili.

At first, nothing. I close the lid and drop the bottle. I should have known, probably nothing more than a crazy lady's herbs. Could I have known? I should have known. I should have bloody known. I punch the pillow and fall into it, exhausted.

Time

And this is how it went. On this day that Baraka came home from school with a dark eye and a face that told a thousand different versions of the same story, on this day that Mama Kabi burned pilau on the stove, on this day I begin again.

They wake up on different sides of the same house with different versions of time past. Kabi, with her head a little heavy, feeling somewhat detached from her body, hears singing in the shower and thinks she is imagining it. Her bed, her covers, her furniture. "Who moved me to my room?"

Smells waft from the kitchen and mum is shouting, "Baraka! You're going to be late for school, get out of the shower!"

Has she finally gone mad? Hearing voices...a coping mechanism? Two minutes later the door is pushed in and there he is with a towel around his waist, hair wet, and the boyish lanky frame barely dried off.

"Sheesh Kabi, you look like you've seen a ghost! It's just eyeliner, what do you think?"

She cannot move and she thinks this is familiar, searching her mind for memory. She thinks this is a dream. Closing her eyes, she whispers, "Not real, not real, not real, not real."

"Kabi, you're freaking me out. Are you okay?Kabi?"

He smells like cocoa butter. A scent she would recognize a kilometre away, attached to him like water to plants on early mornings. She opens her eyes and he is still there, an orange hue finding its way through the window sill, refracting off of his skin where the sun made a love pact with melanin, beautiful light dancing, and she makes a noise that is somewhere between a gasp and a scream. Baraka looks back,

"Muuuuuuuummmmmmmmmmmm! Kabi is acting weird!"

"Baraka, stop disturbing your sister and get ready for school! If the bus leaves you ni shauri yako, I am not going to interrupt my morning to drop you."

He walks towards the mirror in Kabi's room and poses. "Sis, don't make this a big deal okay. I know you said not to touch your stuff but I don't know, I've been feeling kinda weird lately, like low, you know? I just thought trying something different with my look today would make me feel better."

She croaks, "Baraka?"

He looks at her, eyes big and brown, outlined by the black kohl, more precious than anything she has ever encountered and she wants to run to him but she is scared she will reach for him and grab air, scared that he is not really there. So instead she stays still and says, "I love you." Hoping the words will become tangible things that will keep this moment in continuum.

He laughs. Their *I love you*'s are present but more unsaid than said. "I guess the new look does make me more likeable."

"BARAKA, if I have to call you one more time!"

"Yoh, gotta go, Mum's about to break something, or someone." When he reaches the doorway, he turns around. "But just so you know nakupenda pia." And then he is gone.

Okay, she thinks, looks at her phone, notices I am different from what she expected. Thoughts run through her mind. *Okay*, she thinks—hopes?—maybe Baraka dying was just a nightmare? And *this* is what's real? But no, too many days went by.

She collects herself and takes the steps down two by two. She almost trips, steadies herself on the railing, and reaches the last step just in time to catch the conversation taking place in the kitchen.

"Not in my house!"

"Ayii Mum, it's not that big a deal!"

Mama Kabi, never one to consider her words before they come out, says, "What will you be wearing next? Ehh? Lipstick? Dresses? If God wanted me to have another girl, he would not have put that soldier hanging between your legs."

Baraka is mortified. "Muuum!"

"What? It is the truth." She sees her daughter lurking. "Nyokabi, can you talk to this brother of yours. I do not understand what behaviour he is trying."

Kabi stops, her thoughts whirling across her brain. How small this detail is in the scheme of everything, does Mama know he was dead?! Will be dead? But how can she know?

"I swear it is as if God gave me children to punish me. Mwathani, what did I do wrong?! Eeh?! Why do you want my blood pressure to finish?"

Baraka did not expect her reaction to be positive but he expected…well, he does not know what he expected. Just not this, not the overwhelming despair this reaction brings up inside of him. If he had just slipped by unnoticed—but he didn't, and they are here now, and he knows with his mother it is a battle of the will so he tries to reflect strong will on his face but his eyes are glistening.

"Wipe it off."

"But…"

"Now!"

Nyokabi takes the chance to intervene. "Mum maybe…"

"Stay out of this, Nyokabi!"

Kabi works her jaw, measuring her words. "So you only want

me to speak when I am on your side."

Their mother silences her with a look.

Kabi fumes but says nothing.

When he is gone, the black liner sufficiently cleared off his face—another tube stubbornly and comfortably tucked into his pocket, saved for the bathrooms at school—the unfinished conversation hangs in the air between the glances traded back and forth.

"Usiniangalia hivyo, I do it for his own good." Mama Kabi looks at her daughter, about to add something else but changes her mind, busies herself with clearing dishes.

Kabi tries to think of the words to tell her, to explain what is happening, but they do not come. How to say *your son will die by his own hand and I know this because I found his body hanging from the ceiling in the future*— Something clicks. "Mum there is a lady— your second or third cousin, I can't remember her name—she has long dreadlocks and thick arms."

She is distracted. "What are you talking about? Kwanza don't you also need to go to work Kabi?"

"Mum, LISTEN! This is important!"

Mama Nyokabi glares. "Nyokabi, you may be an adult but you do not shout at me under my own roof, ehh?! Remember I still carried you for nine months. Umenisikia?"

Nyokabi restrains herself from throwing something, anything. Deep breaths. "Okay, I just need to know how to find the lady? She's your cousin, the one who always carries cowrie shells."

Mama goes back to cleaning the counter, silent for a moment and then, "Are you talking about Mad-Ma-Nyasi?"

"Who?"

"Mad-ma-Nyasi. Well, she is named Njeri, after our Maitu; we started calling her Ma-Nyasi when…" Mama pauses and drifts off for a minute. "Well, when her daughter died, she left the city for up country, went to live in the grass, and started calling herself a prophetess of God."

She disappears into thought, lost in that space of memory and unspoken words before she remembers she is in the middle of conversation. "Anyway, why do you want to know about her?"

"I just—I just do. Can I get in touch with her?"

"Ha! Does that woman look like she is reachable? I'm even surprised you still remember her. She only comes when she wants to be seen. But that is probably for the best. She carries a bad omen, that one. Anacheza na uchawi."

The dishes cleared, she wipes her hands and moves away. "Anyway I have a chamaa to go to and I suggest if your plan is still to save enough money to leave this house eventually, that you go to work on time before you are fired."

When the house is empty, Kabi calls in sick, and sits in front of her computer, researching.

Google
Potions to go back in time?
Can you change the past?

Medium
How to change the past without a time machine: the Power is Real
Psychology Today
How You Can Alter Your Past or Your Future And Change Your
Present Life
The Philosopher's Magazine
Sorry, Time Travellers: You Can't Change the Past

Kabi skims articles over and over again. Unhelpful papers, essays, conspiracy theorists...until she stumbles on this:

...as Parratt says in Time in Traditional African Thought, time is not an ontological entity. Professor John Mbiti's work around African traditional time centers on the virtual absence of any kind of future. This understanding of time holds for what is present, what has already past and what may naturally occur. This last point is potential time and not necessarily the future. Time in essence then moves backward and not in a forward linear fashion.

What a thing she has found, this Parratt and Mbiti who somewhat understand the way I work and don't work. More and more she reads until she thinks she knows what she must do, and then she starts to feel tired, so so tired. She rests her head, closing her eyes, thinking: it is possible, not tomorrow, not after, only yesterday and now. But I dare say the *what if* cannot always exist in the same realm as the *what is*.

And somewhere on a different side of the city, the *what is* is a boy, is a blessing, a blessing who is moving and breathing and feeling and loving and punching and suffocating and choosing and chasing after what it means to stay alive.

BARAKA

This is how it felt: for a moment, as Kabi drifted off to sleep, she was not here and you were not fully here either—wherever here is for those who exist after life but before forever—you cannot remember how or where, but you were together. You in death and her in life met somewhere in the middle of time where the division had not taken place. And maybe that is why on this morning before your body is to be lowered into a casket, she sleeps with a half-smile on her face. Baba finds her in your room and gently taps her; there are dark shadows on his face and under his eyes but you do not feel guilt or pain for him. "Kabi, sweetie, we cannot be late. Wake up."

Half still in sleep, she asks, "Late for what?"

"Today is the burial."

She yawns and stretches. "What? Which one?"

He clears his throat and repeats himself, "The funeral, mpenzi. We need to get ready to leave."

The expression on her face shifts, she shakes her head. "No, no burial, he is alive."

Baba is terrified; he does not know what to do when his strong collected daughter loses her reason. "It's okay, baby. We all, uhh, we all wish he was still alive, uhm, but today—" he places his palm at the back of his head, rubbing his neck compulsively, "—today let us give him a proper send-off, ehen?"

"No baba, he is alive. I saw him. He was alive."

He holds her, rubbing her back.

"Hush,

   Tsi

     tsi

       tsi,

         Hush.

It was a dream, mpenzi. Be strong now, you have to be strong also for your mother."

Nyokabi's face turns bitter. "That woman can be strong for herself!"

"Ayii yawah, daughter, don't say things like that. I know things have been hard but she is grieving."

"No, she is the reason Baraka was so unhappy. She always looks for a reason to be angry, disappointed."

"As much as I wish I could blame anyone more than myself, Nyokabi, that is just not true. Your mother's responses always have a valid justification."

"That is just her trying to get into your mind. She is always blaming everyone else but herself…"

"Nyokabi, enough."

"And do not think I did not hear her shouting at you. Aren't you also allowed to be in mourning?! You are a grown man! No one, least of all you, should be taking her shit."

"I said enough, Nyokabi!" His voice barely raised but firm. "You will not speak of my wife that way in my house, okay? I know you are angry but today is—today is a day for us to come together, not to fall apart."

Kabi's jaw hardens. "You want to talk about coming together but even you, you were a problem. You and mum both." She shifts her body up, not making eye contact. "You never let him just be himself, everything that made him *him*, you had a problem with. You were afraid he would be one of those boys you and the other fathers gossip about, the ones that bring shame." Her voice cracks. "And now somewhere inside of you there is a sense of relief because you never have to find out."

Rushing of air, palm-on-cheek.

Baba has never touched Kabi before today. How dare he? She holds her face where it is hot and he gasps at what he has done. "Kabi, baby. I'm sorry." He moves to hold her tighter but she pulls away. "You just—" he lifts his hands in exasperation. "You're saying that I wished my son dead. Do you think any parent wishes this for their child? Ehh?"

Kabi does not look at him.

"I would do anything to bring him back, Kabi, believe me— any and every version of him. I didn't understand him but…but God knows I loved him."

"Just—" she whispers, head down. "He was alive." Her eyes well up. "I could have saved him but I didn't."

Baba stands up. "Darling, we all could have saved him, but none of us knew how." He walks toward the door. "Get dressed, I expect you ready in thirty minutes." He sighs. "I know it doesn't feel like it right now, mpenzi, but we will get through this. Somehow, we will get through this."

When he is no longer in the room, Kabi drops to the floor on her hands and knees, frantically searching until she finds it.

The liquid in the bottle is a different colour now, or maybe it is just the way the morning light hits differently. A sip—she tips her head back, her hand stops mid-way and she thinks she must be cautious with it, but, but just one sip. A sip—it burns, burns her tongue, her nostrils, all the way up to her head making it feel heavy. At first: nothing.

Think, she holds the bottle up, remembers *all it needs is time, just give it some time,* and she realizes she is breathing too hard. Brings the bottle back down, forces herself to calm down, to breathe slower.

> Responsible
> > Oldest (as long as she can get to me)
> > Daughter

Dresses in her black trousers and cotton shirt and places the bottle, now half empty, discreetly in the corner of her pocket.

NYOKABI

Baraka used to struggle with history in school. No worries, an easy fix. I loved to narrate stories and Baraka loved to feel stories in his body. With history you could do both.

There was one lesson in particular that wasn't the most interesting for me: Meketilili. We heard it over and over again in school when the teachers were too lazy to research other Kenyan female leaders from our history.

Meketilili had a brother. That's the part they don't really tell you. He was older than her. When we played pretend, Baraka loved this one because he got to be older than me for a little bit. But we never got to the part where Meketilili's brother was kidnapped by Arabic slavers. That wasn't in the picture books, wasn't in the history books.

This is how I know Baraka is not a dream. I have been dreaming of women I do not know. When I wake up, I remember slightly. One of the women is Meketilili. I don't know how I know, but I feel her devastation. It resembles my own. She breathes on me and then smiles.

That is the dream I have before I travel back in time, back to when Baraka is still alive.

TIME

And this is the way it went. On this day when the sounds and the scents of the sea embedded themselves into the two siblings' dark skins. On this day when the sky was an abundant blue. a blue of clarity, a blue that was so sure of itself, nothing save the gravity of the ocean could make it question its sense of being. On this day when the ocean itself teased and danced and showed off its magnitude. On this day when Kabi and Baraka swam in the sea until even the waves were tired. On this day, I begin somewhere.

"Hello? Earth to Kabi! Anyone in there? Yoh, are you even listening to me?"

She blinks, registering where she is and what she is seeing. The air is warm, humid. She can hear waves in the distance. This time she does not hesitate to grab him; this time she draws him in, holding him close; this time when she smells his cocoa butter scent, she kisses his skin until he pushes her away, scrunching up his face, "Ayii, niki?" one of all of the two Kikuyu phrases he can utter.

Nyokabi laughs. "Can't I just appreciate my brother?"

"Not if you weren't listening to me. I swear sometimes it's like I'm talking to a wall with you. Hakuna mtu ndani."

Kabi covers her mouth and fakes a gasp. "Not true! Mimi? A whole me! I always want to hear what you have to say."

He lifts an eyebrow. "Then what did I just say?"

"Uhh…"

"Admit it, you zoned out."

She takes a moment to look at where they are, when they are. A patio. Baraka has an empty plate in front of him. Where they sit, she can feel the coolness of the wooden floorboards under her feet. There are palm trees, and further down, white sand, and further still waves, she can't see them but she can hear them. It clicks: Mombasa.

Baraka, frustrated by his sister, waves his arms up and down. "Hello? Earth to Kabi! Anyone in there? Yoh, are you even listening to me?"

Kabi's gaze falls back on her younger brother. "Haven't we done this part already?"

"Yeah, but you're still not getting the listening to me part right."

She touches his face. "Okay, you got me. I was just distracted by how cute you are."

"Ahh." He smirks. "Now you're just trying to butter me up."

"Is it working?"

"Keep going and we'll see."

Nyokabi laughs, enthralled by all of him. He is tangible,he is here, and she thinks she must find a way to make sure that this time he *stays* here. She kisses his face again.

He pulls away. "Yoh, if you touch me anymore I'll lick you."

"Yuck, Baraka what kind of threat is that?"

"Hey, you're the one breaking all the personal space rules." He moves his chair back, the wooden legs scratching against the patio floorboards. Kabi remembers how much Mum hates it when he does that at home. There are scratches all over the dining room floorboards where he used to drag his chair back. She thinks how silent mealtimes have been recently— *stop thinking.* She is not there; she is here, with him. Baraka, distracted, is oblivious to her momentary silence. "I need to go to the shops." He waves a piece of paper in the air. "Mum gave me a grocery list. Trust her to wait for us to come all the way to the guesthouse and then send me to do the shopping while she sleeps."

Kabi laughs. "God knows African parents have been having children since the beginning of time for the sole purpose of having someone to send around."

"That should be a sermon title," he says. "The calling of African Children to Serve."

"It probably is somewhere." Baraka is already walking away and she calls after him. "Can I come with?"

He turns around and looks at her suspiciously. "Why?"

"I've just missed you is all."

"Mbona, you're being all sentimental today?"

"Ayii, Baraka, stop asking so many questions and just let me come."

"Will you be dramatic about my driving?"

Kabi scoffs. "Between the two of us, who is the dramatic one?"

Baraka raises an eyebrow. "Kabi?"

She lifts her hands up, open palmed in surrender. "Okay, okay. Do you have your license though?"

"I lost it, but I have my abstract."

"Hya basi, twende."

The air is too warm. Kabi rolls down a window, she does not know what is stronger, the thick sea salt smell or the abundant scent of raw fish. And here and there, and now and then, there are certain things that feel moveable, not fully settled. Like sometimes the ground is firm and sometimes the car is gliding over something like water or some other substance that isn't fully formed.

"Sis, are you okay?

Kabi?"

Nyokabi does not realize how much her face gives away. "Huh? Yeah I'm fine I just have a bit of a headache. Which shop are we going to?"

His eyes are on the road—as much as Kabi gives him grief for his speeding, Baraka is a pretty focused driver. "I was thinking Nakumatt, I know they're going out of business almost everywhere but Mum's list isn't long so hopefully we'll find what we need and…"

She stops listening. There is a ringing in her ear. Kabi places her hands on her temple and massages the sides of her head. "Baraka, do you feel that?"

He glances at his sister then looks back at the road. "Feel what?"

"It's like everything is moving."

Baraka chuckles. "That's because we're in a car."

She opens her eyes. She can't see clearly, rubs her temples harder, and closes them again.

"Are you sure you are okay? We can stop the car"

"No. I'm fine. Just a little car sick...aggghhh— "

"Nyokabi?"

She holds onto his arm and just as quickly as it started, it stops. "I'm fine." She is out of breath, gives herself a moment to inhale. "I promise I'm fine." Kabi rolls down the window even lower and draws in the humid air, reminding herself to breathe deep. What is happening? She is fine now but her mind is racing. Baraka does not know, should she tell him now?

"Kabi?"

"Baraka..."

Kabi rubs her arm. "You first."

He inhales sharply. "Whoa! That's so weird."

"What is?"

"Well..." Baraka's eyes are back on the road. He shivers . "This moment. It feels familiar, like...like..."

Kabi asks the same time her brother mutters under his breath. "Deja vu?"

"Deja vu."

Kabi considers Baraka carefully. "Which part?"

He rubs the back of his neck with one hand. "All of it. It's all kind of the same but different, it's just, it's just weird."

Kabi remains silent for a minute, lost in thought. "Remember when we were kids and we used to play all those games? Like—" she pauses and her forehead furrows. "The one, you know it, what's-it-ma-called?"

Baraka is amused by his sister's half memory. "You are going to have to give me more than that to work with, Kabi."

"We gave it a name but I can't remember. It's the game where we would act like we could go back in time and save the day.

Remember there was that one time..."

Baraka asks. "Time travellers?"

"Really?" Kabi laughs. "Is that what we called it? I could have sworn we were more creative than that!"

"Yeah, no." Baraka thinks back. "I would always be the one being saved. Like when we pretended Guka was being attacked by the British soldiers in the forest while he was hiding with Mau Mau, I would be Guka and you would come and say..."

She clears her throat and imitates the deep voice she would put on to make herself sound more serious: "Kimani Kihiu, I am your granddaughter and I am from the future,here to save you from the rotten white men. Come with me."

"Mum used to get so mad at us for messing up the sitting room," Baraka says. "Most of the time it was you who did the messing though, fighting the British soldiers who you somehow decided were all the drapes, cushions, and shawls on the chairs."

Nyokabi half-smiles. "Hey! Don't act like it was all me. You were part of the game too."

The big white mall with the blue almost-but-not-quite neon sign appears. White elephant in the corner, tusks forward in salutation, and the white letters imprinted against the blue backdrop: Nakumatt.

Baraka parks the car and turns off the engine. This journey has been long, short, suspended, unexpected. "I was, but all I did was sit and wait to be saved. You're the one who was always so messy about the saving." And when they laugh, they laugh at each other, and with each other, and for each other.

Kabi does not know where to go from here."I'm from the future and I'm here to save you?"

He unlocks the car doors. "It wasn't that good a line was it? We probably stole it from Star Wars or some shit like that."

"Baraka?"

He keeps laughing as he opens his car door. "Aki we were so unoriginal."

Nyokabi grabs his arm. "Baraka, wait."

He looks back at her and the lightness is gone. "What is it?"

"You're going to die."

He thinks his sister is joking still, though dark humour has never been her strong suit. "Yeah, we all will eventually. Sooner rather than later, if we don't get these groceries to Mum before the sun goes down." He chuckles. "She'll kill us herself."

Kabi looks down, she cannot find the words. "No, that's not what I mean, I just..." And Baraka does not understand the language between words. "Baraka, I just need you to be okay. I need you to be here."

"I am here."

When Kabi looks up, her eyes are watering. "Yeah, you're here now, but I need you to be here tomorrow and the day after that and always."

Baraka takes his sister's hand in his own and squeezes. "Kabi nini mbaya?" He touches her forehead. "You're burning up. Are you okay?"

She wipes a tear and groans softly. "I just..." she chuckles and then sighs and forms the words and then lets them dissipate before they are spoken. "Yeah, it's just the heat. I think it's getting to me a little."

Baraka squeezes her hand. "Hiya basi, tuingie, at least there's air conditioning inside."

And as she gets out she loses her balance, feels dizzy. *Inhale exhale* she tells herself. "Baraka, will you tell me?"

Her brother comes round and takes her arm in his. "Tell you what?"

"If—when, yes *when*, you need help, I need you to tell me."

He laughs. "Kabi, you will know. You always know."

The short walk from the car to the mall is silent. When they are about to enter Baraka asks,. "Can I tell you something?"

Kabi feels like speaking will take too much out of her and she needs to stay here, now. She needs to sit. She nods and leans in closer to Baraka, letting him support more of her weight.

He shifts to better support both of them. "When we were younger and we used to play those games, half of the time I didn't even understand the storyline, world, or time we were playing in. Most of the time you saved me before I even knew I needed saving."

Kabi remembers. She is losing grip of the pavement, she cannot trust the ground. She is tired, so so tired. *No, not now. Not yet.* "Baraka, I think—I think I need to sit."

They walk into a duka that catches Baraka's eye close to the entrance. It is the most inviting one, filled with lesos, beach wraps, deras, blouses, and kanzus of every colour, size, shape, and pattern. There is a little couch near the dressing rooms. Kabi sits. Baraka is mesmerized by the colours and the hues and the waves painted across the clothes in different patterns. He pulls out a bright yellow dera and holds it up against himself, his eyes gleaming. "What do you think?"

Kabi smiles. She wants to tell him he is poetry. She wants to write him into words that never die. "Beautiful," she whispers and then closes her eyes—*just for one moment.*

BARAKA

And this is how to remember, not to remember, to not remember, remember, remember to not, remember not to think about dying. The moment when you started thinking about dying, not the after, not the death, but the act itself. And maybe memory is fiction but remember when Kabi first said it to you.

A joke.

You're going to die.

We're all going to die.

You were not afraid of the after, you were afraid of the process, the act itself, dying. Funny thing, now you cannot remember what it felt like, but memory is fiction, parts of it replaced by imagination to fill in the blanks for what your mind could not process, could not comprehend: numbing, burning, strangulation, heart stopping.

You remember process, the act not the after, but you do not want to remember, you won't remember, can't remember. You want to see, feel, think, how to not think about dying.

Kabi. She is in the car waking up, bottle tucked in the corner of her pockets, numb, silent. You recognize this feeling. And maybe deja vu is not about the specificities, the particularities, but the feeling of a moment repeated in another moment and because memory is fiction you imagine the feeling can only be held in the specificities of the moment. You recognize how she is feeling: tired, afraid, wondering—wandering?

Mum sits next to her, stares out the window. They have not spoken to each other, do not look at each other. Dad drives. Baba always drives; in mourning he will not be driven, even to his own son's funeral he will not be driven. Baba drives even, no, *especially* when everything goes wrong. Both hands on the wheel, never above the speed limit. Maybe that's why you loved to drive fast.

Do not attach memory to feeling but remember Baba sitting in the driver's seat: eyes on the road, stunted conversation, awkward silence. He rubbed the back of his neck with his left palm, right hand gripping onto the wheel so tight you could see his veins through his dark skin.

"So this acting and singing thing, ehh?"

You grunted acknowledgement, already dreading where this was bound to head.

"Your mother told me about the conversation you had," he chuckled. "Baraka, you weren't being serious. Right?"

"What makes you think I wasn't?" you asked.

Dad turned slightly. "Wasn't what?"

"Wasn't being serious."

"Well, that is just not a feasible career."

"I'm good at it."

"Yes, then keep it as a hobby. But to become an actor? A singer? Ati, now you don't want to go to school?"

"It's not that I don't want to go to school, I just don't want to go immediately after I finish my A-Levels. I want to give myself a shot at this thing that I am actually good at."

Baba sighed heavily. "It was already enough stress when Nyokabi wanted to give up her internship at the bank." He raised his free hand, placing air quotations as he spoke, "to pursue writing. Both of you will kill your mother with the decisions you make in a hurry. Huelewi vile tulingangana kulipa school fees? To make sure there was always food on the table? Do you know when you were younger there were months where we did not know where rent was coming from? But we made sacrifices! The things we had to do to pay for those expensive

British system schools of yours? God only knows." He pauses. "You are an adult now, son, you cannot afford to play around with your future *ovyo ovyo tu*. You cannot afford to throw it away."

You could not remember the last time you were honest, truly honest with Baba—unable to bear the disappointment that constantly sits in his eyes when he looks at you these days—but now: "Do you know what it is like for me at school?"

He did not answer.

"*Mimi siyo kama hawa watu wengine,*" you said. "I'm different and they know— "

"No, you are not, son," Baba interrupted. "It's just the stage you are in, okay? A phase. *Ata mimi nakumbuka,* to be a young man in Nairobi is hard. Just give it time. *Utakuwa sawa tu.*"

It is not the same, and you did not know how to explain to him. What he knew and what you have known are different. "Dad, every day I struggle to wake up, to walk, to breathe. This body, it feels wrong somehow like…like I am not capable of carrying it the way I am supposed to. I constantly have to lay down one part of myself to survive and it's exhausting. The only place I feel seen, the only place I feel heard, the only place I feel *safe* is when I am on stage, and I can be anyone or anything but myself."

Baba pursed his lips. "I want your grades up this term. And then at the end of the term we will go and speak to Mr. Rotich about applying to universities. He said you're really good at math. If you just applied yourself you could get into an engineering program."

"You've never seen me perform," you said softly.

Remember, eyes on the road. You know he is thinking of you. Thinking of all the ways he could have been different for you so that you would be different for him.

Memory is fiction but four years old and Mama used to call you her second girl. She said you would hold onto her skirt tighter than misty air holds onto water. Eight years old and Kabi fought a boy in the neighbourhood for calling you a girl. That's when you learned you were wrong somehow. Twelve years old you liked a girl, she didn't like you back. Fourteen years old you had a best friend, his name was Vic; he taught you how to be a boy. Fourteen years old you liked a boy, but you never said it out loud, you never even thought it in public. Fifteen years old, boy moved away. Sixteen years old you prayed to be different and you prayed and you cried and you realized you were a problem. Seventeen years old you couldn't sleep and you smiled in public and you hurt in private and you asked God to make it all stop, this farce. Memory is fiction but you stayed alive. You did stay, you stayed alive you did, stay alive you stayed.

Until you couldn't anymore.

NYOKABI: EULOGY

"**B**araka used to say that one of the reasons we are here is for here and now. He advocated for fully living in the present moment and I…"

Can't finish. Tears close my throat. A sob comes out on stage in front of this collection of friends and strangers. I've been better about holding my tears, keeping them for when I am alone but not now.

"I just—I just can't talk about the here and now without talking about yesterday." There is mucus running from my nose and the weight of this grief will bring me to the ground. I look at Mum but her eyes are hidden behind dark shades and even though I can't see them, I feel her gaze elsewhere. My hands shake almost as much as my voice. "I can't talk about the here and now without talking about the absence that exists in tomorrow."

Yesterday tomorrow, yesterday tomorrow, yesterday tomorrow. I close my eyes and he is there behind my lids in the darkness, I see him, and I curse him and I want to say, *How dare you make me write your eulogy?*

But instead I say pretty words. "God's timing and Baraka means blessing and I…"

Can't finish. Suddenly there are arms around me and I think it is him but I open my eyes and it is Baba and I fall into him and

I stop pretending that I have the energy to be strong and I wail into his shirt and he takes the half open silver notebook in my hand and reads on my behalf and I am led to a chair to sit and I close my eyes and I count to ten times one hundred, fiddling with the bottle in my pocket, and I remind myself how to breathe and I open my eyes and wish I didn't have to so I draw it up to my lips and swallow. It is more than halfway gone; let me go with it.

This time I can save him, I know I can.

This time he will stay alive.

BARAKA

This is how to not think about being alive when you are dead. Do not watch the living. Do not attach memory to feeling.

Do not attach memory to feeling but of the things that reminded you what it means to be alive.

Music. Sound and rhythm interrupting silence long ago taught you how to move:

ta tadata ta-ta

ta tarata ta-ta,

ta-tarata-ta-da.

Do not attach memory to feeling but remember the time Kabi surprised you with your first Blankets and Wine concert tickets and on that day in the middle of April when the clouds threatened to interrupt every outdoor plan, you prayed.

You didn't pray to be different and you didn't pray to be better and you didn't pray to be other and all you prayed was that it wouldn't rain and that you would get to listen to Sauti Sol play. But sometimes prayers are like music, and sometimes someone listens and is moved, so this time, unprecedented, the sun teased its way out of hiding and this time the grass was greener on *this* side and this time you stood with Kabi out under the rainless sky and sang Lazizi word for word at the top of your lungs and this time you let the music carry you and you took Kabi by the hand—just this once, she said—and you laughed and you danced until even the ground was tired of holding you up.

Do not attach memory to feeling, do not watch the living, but as you watch her swallow the liquid that burns her tongue, you think: *she is coming to find me, somewhere between life and after, in the middle of time, she is coming to find me.*

TIME

And this is how it went. On this day when Baraka thought of his mum's burnt pilau, on this day when he first really considered, not just thought—many people tease the thought—but really considered what it would look like to die, I begin somehow. Here they are at their destination, no, at *a* destination. *Their* would imply intention and traveling through me will not, cannot, demand a particular space or place.

"Here is fine." Baraka has been dreading this moment, does not want to be seen here, now—today is one of those days where he does not want to be seen anywhere, wishes he could temporarily exist in non-visibility and come back only when he is ready.

Nyokabi looks at her brother perplexed. "Where are we?" Her hands are on the wheel, Dad's car, but this time it is harder to orient herself to her surroundings, senses lagging behind, tumbling over each other one after the other in an attempt to catch up with her consciousness.

Sound: Afternoon birds chirping, laughter, greeting—
Buudaaaaaah— boys shouting in close distance.

Tongue: Mouth dry, throat parched, tingling far-off taste—
pili-pili.

Skin: Cool air, soft breeze, wisps of kinky hair escaping turban and falling onto her face.

Scent: Something burnt…where is that coming from? Like rice on a stove that has been left too long.

Eyes: Big colonial-style buildings, red bricked constructions bearing architectural memory of a borrowed land that now houses education taught in a borrowed language. White lines on the grey pavement demarcating space to say *from here until here.* Parking lot of Baraka's high-school. Baraka lost in thought, she knows the way he is now is not the way he was before. His eyes dart across space as if he and not she is the one lost in time.

Baraka misses her question or hears but does not register or hears and registers but does not respond. He gets out of the car, backpack slung over shoulder, oversize T-shirt, saggy shorts, and sports shoes with one lace falling off the side of his left shoe.

That will trip him up.

"Baraka, your laces." Kabi moves swiftly into action when she feels like she is finally fully here; unclipping her seat belt and opening her car door just before he takes a step and trips—as predicted— but catches himself before the ground gets the chance to.

"Huh?" He looks down. "Ohh yeah." Gets down on one knee and lets his bag slip to the ground as he bends to tuck the loose lace back into his shoe. Kabi reaches out her hand to pull him up. He doesn't take it.

"What's up, Baraka?"

"Nothing." He pushes himself off the ground and avoids his sister's gaze.

Kabi searches herself for the right words. "Baraka…"

"Kabi I don't want to talk about it. I'm already late for basketball practice as it is. Don't wait, I'll find my way home."

She understands, maybe? She thinks she does. He hates sports. How to not lose him. She grabs his arm and holds his gaze. "Or you could just not go today?"

"If I skip one more day of practice, Coach will kick me out of the team and Dad won't let me perform in the musical this term. I have to go, Kabi."

"Okay." But Kabi is thinking fast. "Then I am going in with you and I will wait until you are done and we can go home together."

He rubs the back of his neck, a nervous tick he picked from Dad. "Nyokabi, I just don't know how much of a good idea it is…me showing up to practice with my sister, you know?"

"Ha! Are you embarrassed of me?"

He looks away. "It's not that."

"Then what, Baraka?"

He does not answer.

Kabi tries to hug him, to draw him in, but he does not budge. *Where are you, kaka? Do not withdraw.* She purses her lips. "I am coming, Baraka. Unless you are physically going to stop me, I have made up my mind."

"Just try not to draw attention to yourself."

"Me?" She smiles. "Never"

He rolls his eyes; a little smile —*progress*— "Mmmhmm."

As they enter the court, a stocky boy, two inches shorter than Baraka with light skin and a bruised cheek, yells, "Oya, look who it is! Little princess pussy and his what?" The boy looks Kabi up and down. "Babysitter?"

Another boy: *Max?* Kabi thinks —she's seen him around every once in a while— chimes in. "That's his sister, man!"

The shorter brown boy whistles. "Baraka, you never told us your sister was so fine. Tell her to come through, tutamuonyesha vile boiz huweka dame!"

Baraka steps in front of Kabi. "Shut up, Ian."

The boy walks up to Baraka. "Or what, princess? Utado? Usisahau vile nilikushow last time."

A whistle blows and the coach's voice rings through the stadium. "Cool it, Nindaba!"

Ian smiles, still looking at Baraka. "Just burning off a little steam, Coach. Nothing serious."

Then he says lower, "Usithaani nimesahau vile nilipata hii." He points to the purplish bruise on his right cheek. "Tukona biashara hatujamaliza."

Kabi's blood is boiling. This must be the boy who has been making her brother's life hell. She steps out from behind Baraka. "Is that a threat?"

The boy smirks. "Nothing you need to worry your pretty face about. Your brother and I just have guy things to catch up on."

Every fiber of her being is revolted by this. She points at him, moving closer as she speaks. "Listen, you are nothing but a scared little asshole with a big ego trying to compensate for your lack of bigness anywhere else."

Baraka touches her shoulder. "Kabi, leave it."

But she ignores him. "Don't you ever speak to my brother with any inflection or intention of offence, ever! If you even *look* at him funny again, I will..."

"You'll what?" Ian looks half amused.

"Nyokabi!" Baraka is holding onto her shoulder tighter now. His look shuts her up, and she closes her fists hard, fingernails digging into palms. She walks towards the bleachers and sits, pursing her lips.

Whistle-blows. Start—the team:

divided,
shuffling, grunting,
screeching of sneakers
sliding across wooden panels

Sweaty bodies
connecting-dis

        connecting,
folding over knees,
panting, inhaling deep, exhaling fast

THUMP

Baraka is on the ground, Ian standing over him. It happened so quickly there's no evidence of anything other than the latter offering his hand to pull the former up. "You better be careful princess. These floors are slippery. Someone could hurt themselves really badly."

"Foul!" Nyokabi screams from the bleachers.

The coach silences her with a look. "Last I checked this was my court, young lady, not yours, and I would prefer it if you didn't speak for or to what happens during practice."

"But coach, my brother—"

"Your brother is my player first and foremost until 60'clock. You can decide what he is after that."

He turns back to the boys who are all silent and still, some of them using this moment to catch their breath. "Are you good, Kim?" He refers to Baraka by his last name as he does with all the boys.

"Yeah, yeah, I'm fine." Baraka is already up off the ground but he is cradling his right shoulder and wincing, ignoring the snickering coming from Ian's direction.

The coach turns to Ian. "Take a bench, Nandabi."

Ian quickly begins his protests. "But Coach, come o—"

The coach turns his attention back to Baraka. "Do you want to sit the rest of this out?"

When Coach's gaze lands on him, Baraka releases his arm, letting it fall by his side. Nyokabi notices his face tightening.

"Yeah, I'll be fine."

Kabi knows he won't. "Coach, surely you can't let him play like that."

Coach doesn't look at her. "As much as I do not like being told what I can and cannot do with *my* team on *my* time in *my* court, Kim, I must agree with your sister. Go home, sleep the injury off."

"Coach—"

"Don't come back until you can move your arm without twisting your face like a hare caught in a trap." Coach whistles and turns back to the other boys. "Hya! I'm sure you have all been highly entertained! Back to it!"

Nyokabi is already down the steps but Baraka walks past her without saying a word. As they open the door to leave, Coach calls after them. "Maybe leave the spectators at home until the actual games, ehh?"

Ian says something and the other players chuckles. Nyokabi is fuming but too worried to react. "Should we go to a hospital?"

He does not respond. They get to the car.

Beep.

Unlock, doors pulled open, closed shut, seat belts buckled,

engine turned on, windows drawn down.

"Baraka?"

He looks straight ahead. "Let's just go home."

And she knows she does not have time but he knows that time doesn't matter now and he wants to not be seen, to not be heard, tired of using his voice in any capacity. And so they drive in silence to a destination, their destination?

Home—a place or people. Mama and Baba are out visiting. Mum left a note on the kitchen counter:

Food in Sufurias.
Wash dishes after. Nawapenda.

Baraka walks straight to his room and locks the door behind him. Nyokabi calls out, and now and then and here and now she is barraged by blinding pain behind her brow and she wants to cry and to sit and to sleep and to not wake up but she knows she is already sleeping and she is already tired so she will wake up.

She follows her brother and sits in the hallway leaning against the closed door of his room, back of head resting on the wooden frame. "Baraka, talk to me."

Baraka sits on the other side of the door struggling to breathe. He looks around him for something to hold onto. His arm is throbbing, *focus on that.* The pain means he is still here, parts of him moving inside him. He is exhausted and cannot explain it. She won't understand.

"Baraka please?"

"You can't save me," he says softly.

Kabi's heart beats faster, louder, in her ears—intensifying the growing migraine. "What?" she whispers. *Does he know?*

He raises his voice. "You don't get to always save me, Kabi!"

"I just…it's that boy isn't it? Ian, he's such an ass. I'm going to tell Mum to talk to the administration about getting him expelled."

"No!" Baraka hits the back of his head against the door. "You see, you're not even listening! You don't listen. No one ever listens."

"Okay, okay." Nyokabi massages her temples. The tiredness is growing but she will not let herself go. "Tell me, Baraka, please. I want to listen, I am listening."

Baraka doesn't hear his sister's taut tone, focuses on trying to get the words from his mind to his mouth. "Kabi, I am not something to be fixed, you know?"

"I never said you were—" she stops herself, *listen listen listen.*

"You've always made it your responsibility to save me. Always making decisions for me—speaking on my behalf—you never gave me room to just—to just fucking *be,* Kabi." He goes quiet.

"Baraka, I've only ever wanted to protect you. I'm your older sister."

"Yes, but I have two parents! I never needed a third; I am not one of your bloody projects! Have you seen how Dad looks at me? I know he wishes I was different. God, I wish I was different! Everything I do is a disappointment.

"And mama? She doesn't know what to do with me. Every time she sees me, like truly sees me, I see the confusion in her eyes. And then there's you, Kabi.

"I can't stand the way you give me those woiye looks as if there is something damaged in me, something that needs to be solved, to be fixed."

He bangs his head against the door and Kabi on the other side covers her mouth, the heaviness of his words settling in her body. Calling on this love that holds them, she is exhausted from how much it takes to remain in this moment. *Does he actually believe this?*

"I just wanted," Kabi's body is shutting down but she forces herself to get the words out, "I wanted to protect you." She closes her eyes, the pain and exhaustion pulling her into the realms of darkness and dreaming and waking and day. But just before she does she hears choppy bits of his response.

"…not your job."

TWO

TIME

And it is not my turn to tell this part of the story but here something must be understood: some stories cannot be told while they are happening to the people telling them—because they are happening only in fragments.

A little bit from here:

Nyokabi screaming at a burial. Not the shouts of the mourning but the shouts of brutalization as if the body is being chewed out.

A little bit from there:

Hush. Ayii, why is her child disturbing the silence?
Mama Nyokabi does not understand why she must console when she is the one who has lost a child.

A little bit from where?

Baba Nyokabi embarrassed at the scene, guilty for feeling embarrassed, also scared…and what does a man do with his fear in mourning?

NONI KIMANI

You have not known pain until you have had your child put in the ground before you. Watching them bury his body feels like…it feels…feels like a thousand blunt pangas cutting different parts of my skin all at once but slowly. Not deep cuts, shallow enough that no vein is touched so that I stay alive to feel the pain.

They dig and dig and dig.

The pangas cut and cut and cut and cut.
Lower the Casket

They bury and bury and bury

I bleed and bleed and bleed.
But of course they do not see.
And today I refused to look at my baby's body.
Si yeye.
It is not him. They said it would give me closure, said it would be a last goodbye but did they see him hanging from the ceiling with a shuka I had worn around my waist wrapped around his neck?

Hanging as if he was floating—flying? When you looked at his feet—only his feet. But no, they did not have to move their eyes up from his feet up, up, up his too thin legs, up, up, up to his broad, still dark, shoulders to his still beautiful face.

No, no, no. I do not have to see him again. His body is not *closure*, not him, not goodbye. Can never be goodbye.

And now she is shouting as if she has been possessed; this other child of mine that I am furious with, this one that I found sitting there against the wall, frozen. The picture is ingrained into my mind, the silence, and now she screams.

Nini mbaya na yeye?

I am a bad mother. I think, *and scared.*

I know I cannot lose two children but at the same time, I do not have the strength to be a mother to only one without the other.

TIME

I will tell the history of storytellers who carried me within them.

Hadithi hadithi

Njoo Njoo

A quick lesson in history:

And here and there and now and then there was Njeri, one whom our Ma Nyasi, Mama Kabi's "second or third cousin," is named for. Kabi and Baraka's mother's father's mother's mother, referred to in stories only as Maitu Njeri. And this is where the lines converge, ahh, yes, full circle. Ma-Nyasi and Mama Kabi's shared Maitu was a medicine woman

& herbalist

& healer

& body worker

& scientist

& doctor

and whatever other words given by language to name the work of conversing with the body.

Hya, hya. Let's go back. 1920s Kenya, thirty or so years before the 1950s colonial Kenya which would be re-enacted almost half a century later by eleven year old Kabi and nine year old Baraka.

But that was the play pretend.

In one version of the real story, Maitu Njeri is one of the ones who condemn the coming of the white man, like others before and around her. They preached of: snakes and jacaranda trees, skin the colour of porridge, death, theft, and a God that required closed eyes when praying to him. Blindness.

Before the 1920's Maitu Njeri heard whispers that the prophetess Mekatilili had slapped a white man. That she'd called on the ancestors to avenge her, had danced freedom and been deemed insane. Was exiled but came back. Was exiled again. When the prophetess Mekatilili died in 1914, Maitu Njeri's work became more urgent. Not only bodies needed healing; now the land was also crying out, defiled with innocent blood.

Aki aki yawah! *Aki the land*! Maitu cried for the earth, communed with the ancestors, picked things in pieces to prepare for what was to come.

A root from here,

                                                 Leaves from there,
              thabai cannot be forgotten, the stinging nettle,
Aha, and what about that colourful one?
Sitting like a purple flower?

   Maitu had never seen it before, but there it lay and her eyes
remained steady —focused—guided to what was being offered
                            by the earth:
                       something to heal,
                       something to save.

                 The gift of myself, time.

   It is not my turn to tell this part of the story…

MA NYASI

This one I will tell because time is not always reliable. Time will make you forget that some things hurt as deeply as they did, deed, dead. Time will turn that hurt into numbness and selective amnesia. Mimi, I've refused! It happened in the early 2000s, this thing that changed me irrevocably. "Time will heal," they say, "time will tell."

Ha! Does death not still hang in the air with me now?

When the doctors told me my Sifa was dead, it was said just like that.

"She is dead."

No roundabout, *you know's…* and *what happened was…* No softening of the blows, no trying to appease the mother. She was alive and now she is dead.

Just like that.

There in that hospital with the white white walls and the pictures of the white white missionary nurses carrying black black babies, dark like my baby Sifa. Not baby, she hates it when I call her baby.

Hated it when I called her baby.

Just about to graduate with a bachelor's degree in engineering.

So different from me; her father was the one who liked math and technical things—her father who left me when she was three. Not for any particular reason, just because he could.

When they told me she was dead, I touched my tongue to the roof of my mouth and sucked the saliva. From the moment I heard about the car accident, something steeled me for this. Nilikuanajua tu. And so I did not cry or wail like the way mothers are expected.

Ah-ah! Me, I grasped the little key hung on a chain around my neck for support and I nodded my head as the doctor told me she was dead. The accident itself had not killed her, but she did not get to the hospital in time to be saved; Kenyan ambulances are not fast to come. The doctor tried not to say it like that but I understood what was there between the words spoken. Still, I was calm. I nodded my head and called my one brother to come and help me sign papers.

I did not cry. I did not flinch. I was calm.

As we planned the funeral, I called Baba Sifa and he did not pick up. I did not call again. I had done my part. If a man could not be present for his daughter in life, what right had he to be there in death anyhow? Over the next few days, I started making my peace with his unsurprising absence—I chastised the part of me that had the audacity to hope he would show up even—and then by and by he did.

Baba Sifa heard it longhand; the news making its way from one of the cousins back in Central whose husband was travelling to Nanyuki for business, and on that business trip, lo and behold, who does the husband run into but Baba Sifa himself, doing God only knows what there. That was how this man—acting as if he was even more entitled to this grieving than I was—heard of his daughter's death.

And still, he did not call me. I did not even know anything about his whereabouts until the cousin's husband got back home and told her to tell me that he had run into my ex-husband. We were never married. Not worth correcting.

I remember the looks from that time, not the faces. There are so many faces after death: cousins, aunties, uncles, friends—you cannot remember which one is which— but I do remember how they looked at me.

ayiii is this a mother really?

see ata she's not even crying

what mother does not weep after their daughter has died?

Both my parents died when I was still a child. Maybe I had resigned myself to the fact that this type of loss would follow me always. Or maybe the looks held truth: evidence of an insanity that was creeping into my bones. But I could not, did not want to recognize it. Then Baba Sifa came back to Nairobi.

Where had he been? they wondered. He did not say. I did not ask. Yet automatically everyone started looking to him for direction for Sifa's funeral.

I suppose that may have been when the insanity seeped in. Watching this man, who left two decades ago, come back and act like he had been part of my daughter's life. I don't know— maybe insanity is just unexpressed anger. I don't know...maybe.

I started having dreams. Dreams of Sifa, Sifa as a baby, Sifa when she got her acceptance into UON. Sifa here, Sifa there, interspersed with dreams of Cucu and her stories of time, stories that could not be fully grasped in a dream retelling:

There's me; a little girl sitting on Cucu's lap and she's telling me about her mother—Maitu Njeri— the traveller whose name I carry. Cucu, whose memory is not reliable, remembers this story clearly. This story about thabai and a purple flower and an earth that could not be healed. And a locked wooden box with the key on a chain around Cucu's neck. I am pointing to this box and she says, "Not yet. Sometime but not now."

Sifa interrupts my dream, saying, "I am still here. Come find me."

And for days I could not forget that little box. The story of thabai and purple flowers teased memories out of the recess of my mind. And for days every time I closed my eyes I found myself traveling through these different women: Cucu, Maitu, Sifa, myself. And I knew they could not bury my baby.

When I realized this I thought for sure that I was the one going mad but no, for the first time that I was experiencing clarity like I had not experienced before. And maybe madness is clarity.

Haraka haraka,
haina baraka

My grandmother's favourite saying. Everything happens in the time it is supposed to happen. So this is how it went: on the day of the funeral I stumbled upon the box. I say stumbled because I was not really looking for it, but I was expectant; nilijua tu somehow it would find me. And there it was, as if it had always been there. In the glass cabinet of our family home in central Kenya—where Cucu raised me after my parents died, where they were both buried— where Sifa would be buried.

I could hear it calling me. Not the box—the thing inside it. I could smell so many different things from within: sweet and bitter, sour, salty, honey, savoury, pungent, thick, but also soft, lingering. The past and the future.

The smell of time is heavy.

Do you know what happens when a thing is found which is not supposed to exist? Madness. Insanity. I have always preferred the word madness to insanity; it feels more rooted, more tied to the ground. Insanity ends in an unfinished sound, *eeeeee*, like you are waiting for the word to close but it remains open. At least with madness, there is a sense of finality. A kissing of tongue to teeth. *Assssiii.*

The word they had for my mother was schizophrenia. Assssiweeeee! That one is a word that goes on so long, you don't even know where it begins or ends. Schizophrenia-schiz-ophrenia-schizo-phrenia. Too many letters wasted. This language we were forced into does not know how to conserve.

It wastes too much in words. And yet, they had no words for my father, him who loved both men and women. A fact he tried to conceal from everyone, even himself, into his marriage. Unakumbuka Kenya in the 60s?

Kenya in the 60s: decades before the virus began spreading faster than it could be understood. Kenya in the 60s: a decade when the country won its independence, became a republic, and enacted a system of democracy with its own president. Kenya in the 60s: a decade where my mother's madness and my father's sickness were inconsequential to the history being made. I've been told that when my father infected my mother with the virus, her visions became worse. They would find her muttering to people who were not there, and when asked she would say only, "You are the ones imagining that I am imagining," and carry on with her conversations, eyes glassy.

Three weeks after she gave birth to me, she dropped me at Cucu's house and left. They found her naked and drowned in the dam, thirty kilometres away. Cucu said I was lucky; lucky because I had escaped the virus, lucky because I was alive. Schizophrenic. That's what the doctors called my mother. Cucu told me she would never let them put her in those institutions of theirs. "We are from proud ancestry!" I would hear, over and over again.

Her own mother, Cucu said, had been called mad to invalidate her freedom words. But of all the stories she told me, I think this was the one she could never tell fully, all at once. She could only ever hold a few pieces of the story in her hands at a time, never the whole. I think that it is a wound she carried to her grave.

If she had let them take my mother to hospital, would she still be alive?

Madness is lonely. But it is not madness if it is real.

After he found out about his wife's death, my father took off his shirt and his trousers, wailing in his half naked state. He did not come to take me from Cucu. I wonder if he considered it, maybe turned around to walk towards me, and then changed his mind? Of all the times I've lived through, I refuse to go back to this one. Because I do not really want to know.

They said he ran off with a man he met in the bar who also had the virus. He came home to die when I had already left for Nairobi. I did not go home to watch him die, I did not consider it. For me, he died when my mother died. Any version of him after that was not my father. And time cannot tell this story because time makes you believe that it happened long ago, as if I do not carry it with me now.

As if I did not carry the madness of the women before me in my bones—the clarity that started as a prickly feeling in my gut the day of Sifa's funeral—on that day I opened the box with the key around my inherited chain.

Clarity spread, warm and slow throughout the rest of my body, assured of itself. A strong and soft everything-scent tickled the back of my throat as I reached inside to touch the colourful assortment of herbs and leaves.

Uwwwiiii!

Tears filled my eyes, my finger burning. *Asssiii*, the stinging nettle of course. I should have been more careful. At that moment I noticed the little jar on the side of the box with a purplish liquid inside. The purple flower! I knew, I knew, I knew, as I lifted it up and pulled the lid off the bottle: I knew I was opening time.

TIME

B ut here I am telling this fragment…

And this fragment.

And this is how it went:

Nyokabi is still. One to ten times one hundred, then she counts in ten, twenty thirty, forty, fifty, sixty seconds tick tocking their way into the lowering of the casket. It is the calm before the storm—before the madness—before the clarity—

Before she interrupts the stillness. There it is now, the deep heavy guttural sound building, rising from her lungs. A sound so heavy that everything is stopped. It is not a crying of sadness, it is not a weeping of mourning.

It is angry, volatile, violent.

The mangled sound moves in a zig zag way, up and down and in and out. words and syllables not making sense until Nyokabi finally forces them into cohesiveness. "You will kill him! Don't! He is alive! He won't come back!" And she is shouting and running and grieving, arms outstretched towards the grave waiting for her—caught midway—

And here is the problem with the grieving going mad

in public: nobody is sure how much madness is warranted.
How much becomes too much? A cause for concern? There
is a certain level that is acceptable, yes, but surely there must
be a line somewhere where it gets crossed? Before it gets
uncomfortable...

So amidst the crowd there is shifting from one leg to the
other, and murmurs as some are remembering—not all—but
a few here and there are finding this scene familiar. Originally
enacted by another woman decades ago.

Isn't it that one who is the mother's cousin?

Ahh this family surely.

Can they not just grieve like normal people?

Ni shatani. Weh! He has really come into this family.

But of course these are not things that could be asked or
said out loud, so they remain locked in the thoughts of those
gathered—out of respect—to be reopened for speculation later,
after sufficient time of mourning has passed that gossip could be
had without too much guilt.

Aha yes! The ones regretting what made them make the trip all
the way from Nairobi—when there was no accommodation!—
are appeased. They have a story to carry back. This is how they
maintain their charitability in their tiredness: by imagining who
will want to be filled in on what and when. *Mmmhmm yes!* Those
tantalizing speculations.

"*I heard the boy was not right in the head either.*"

"*Ayiii tsi! No wonder he... you know...*"

"*Niliskia ata that woman, you know the one who is a cousin?*"

"*Mad Ma Nyasi?*"

"Yes, the mad one! I heard even her mother died from madness ati."

"Ehee! Really? Woiii, poor Ken. Did he know he was marrying into a family of madness?"

"Ahh that one, even his father was an alcoholic."

"Weh! We must pray for them. This family, ni kama Shatani alikua na shida na wao."

Fragments of speculations, gossip, prayer requests? Those, they thought together but separately. Not for now. At least here there is a silent consensus.

For now, they watch the madness repeat itself in the grieving daughter, being held by her father, as the shouts turn to whimpers, and then to mutterings. She is unseeing. Someone asks to move her, but any movement, any attempt to touch her other than her father's, triggers the screaming.

And the mother is there also, standing still, her face like stone. Strange, they wonder, that she does not go to comfort her grieving daughter. The gathered mourners cannot see her eyes underneath the dark shades she wears, but she seems unbothered. They follow her lead: slightly relieved, slightly disappointed.

A sense of expectancy pulsates the atmosphere in the wake of Kabi's shouting.

He is alive! He is alive! Do not kill him!

Something about the stating of the impossible so certainly, so angrily, settles in the air, building up, waiting for an eruption of sorts—a Lazurus moment?—only to be stilled, cut short by a mother's cold glance. So them—the gatherers—mutter thoughts not supposed to be spoken too loudly, wanting to place their nervous energy.

Isn't it the mother who should be going mad anyhow?

Needing to speculate,

This seeing dead people is….

Yes, tamu tamu speculations. In fragments.

Uchawi. Yes, the work of the devil I tell you.

And the mother herself is being watched by the mad woman. When their eyes meet, Mama Nyokabi wonders, *Has she always been here?* This woman from so long ago…it always comes back to this.

Full circle.

In fragments.

This land carries both their histories and now both their dead.

An understanding passes between them, this shared knowing of losing a child, of watching them dig the soil and cut your flesh: shovel, dirt, slice, skin, fracture you deeper and deeper but not deep enough that the veins are touched, so you must stay alive to feel everything. The madness appearing in different ways.

When Sifa—Ma Nyasi's daughter—died, Mama Nyokabi paid her obligatory respects at the funeral, changad for the funeral fundraiser, and moved on with her life. When she heard of the woman's madness, she *tsk'd tsk'd* and moved on. Except… except for that one time. None of her concern, she thought, this woman who had gotten herself pregnant by a man she had no business being with, a man who left at the first signs of trouble. Truth be told, Mama Nyokabi had been scared, scared of the tragedies that followed their family. She did not want to be associated with that…none of her business, she convinced herself, every time after that one time. And now here she was, reliving what Njeri had lived.

Someone is saying a blessing over the mound of earth and that is it.

Dust to dust,

Ashes to Ashes.

Mama Nyokabi looks over the ground that covers her son's body then looks back at the mad woman. There is no empathy or kindness in her gaze or body movement. There is just the knowing, and Mama Nyokabi exhales a shuddering release of air she did not know she had been holding in. She walks away from the grave site, her best friend Ciru at her heels tittering and tattering.

Baba Nyokabi, holding his mumbling daughter, notices his wife leave from the corner of his eye. Fear. What does a man do with his fear in mourning? *She cannot leave,* he thinks. *What do you do when the ones you are supposed to protect leave?*

And here is where his embarrassment lies as his daughter says, "I can bring him back." Softer now: "He is…not gone."

The tension built up by her madness now dissipating, the gatherers become antsy, some walking away in pairs. Apologetic glances and *Look at the time,* written all over their faces. The journey back to Nairobi is long. Everything is calming back down for them but for Baba Kabi the explosion is not done with.

It is an eruption in process, slow—wife's back turned, quiet—daughter muttering,

Responsible-oldest-daughter

over and over;

He is still Alive

And this is where his embarrassment lies:
His inability to protect,
to provide—vows he made—twenty five years to date;
to love, to keep safe—twenty two years to date;
He glances at the cross that holds his son's name—
to keep alive—nineteen years to date;
At the very least to keep alive, Goddamnit! The bare minimum, a vow that went unsaid, that followed the love and protect and provide—*to keep alive.* A failure, like his own father.

And this is where his embarrassment lies.

They are singing songs about eternity. He wishes he could live in the words of hymns. And he is embarrassed at this thought—

that still he wants to run away. What kind of man is he? He feels his daughter trembling, but the storm has passed.

Ashes to ashes,

Dust to Dust.

She is still now. He loosens his grip and realizes the shakiness comes from his own body. He catches the gaze of an unfamiliar woman. Who is this woman without shame? This one who will not let him have his grief unobserved? Of course those gathered tend to stare at the family in mourning after death but their gaze is more shallow. She does not look away from their madness.

Baba Nyokabi does not want to consider that for now. The history of madness. His own father not having the language to name what he had struggled with. In today's world it would have been called depression but when Baba Nyokabi was a boy, sadness without reason was not a thing to talk about. When something cannot be understood it cannot be explained, so instead of talking about it, his father drank himself into oblivion. A story that Kenneth Kimani had wanted to keep away from his children, a history to protect them from, but now see

Look how history repeats itself. The past carries itself into the present, resisting amnesia, recreating what it was in multiple different ways. The woman walks towards him, a past walking into his now, clicking and calling. He remembers the story his wife told him about the woman whose madness came after the death of her daughter.

Aha!

This one who says she speaks for me. He has nothing to say to her.

Nyokabi, who is lost between the here and now and then and there, has not stopped whispering under her breath:

"My

    Mine."

Stunted words.

"Gone…

Here."

Fragments removed from any meaning given context. When they place the last mound of soil on Baraka's grave, all the sound dissipates. *They killed him*, she thinks. She should have jumped inside, stopped them.

What good would that have done? Reason asks her, but she locks it away.

He was alive.

Was, is alive,   alive,
   a life,   alive,
      he was,   alive,
         he is,   alive,
           is he,   alive,
            life lost?

Dust to dust,

                   Ashes to ashes.

And then she sees mama's cousin, second or third? The mad woman, Ma Nyasi, walking towards them. She knows. Kabi interrupts her own muttering; she attains clarity.

"You," Kabi says. "Tell them."

"Wasted tears," the woman *tsks tsks* at her. She turns to Baba Kabi. "Go after Noni."

He is taken aback by his wife's first name. Not Mama Nyokabi, or Mama Baraka, not your wife: Noni. Her sense of familiarity. It was deliberate and it works. He looks at his daughter and back at the mad woman but she nods reassuringly. He thinks about Noni walking away, what it felt like, this small action. He turns hurriedly, in his embarrassment, in his fear, he walks in the direction which she went.If he does not find his wife now they may never find each other again.

The gatherers are dispersing, following Tata Ciru's lead— as always—who directs them to the tents where some tea is prepared for those who have managed to stay the service through until the end. Most city dwellers have already left and when the ones who haven't realize that it is not a second lunch or an early dinner being served but a little cup of too-milky-too-sugary tea in tin mugs, they will leave as well, carrying stories of the eventful burial, checking and rechecking versions of the story to revise for later rehashing. Bits and pieces.

A little here.

A little there

A little where?

That family ayiyayaya. We must pray for them

Of course they will be devastated when they say these things

Ehhheee, truly they need God's providence

Hehh! And Let me tell you the way that boy went…

And they will bring the conversations round to themselves

Unajua sikuhizi with everything that our children are being exposed to, ah, we must be very careful.

Weh! Hapo kwanza wanaume! We have to protect our boys.

Did I tell you about my friend Christine and her son Ian?

No. Hebu tell me.

Apparently he has been to rehab three times.

Mara tatu? Wacha!

Imagine! These children mayo! I am really scared for this generation.

Heh yenyewe, they will be the death of us...

And Baraka will get lost in the names of those who are still alive,
becoming a memory, a warning, a lesson,
this forgotten blessing.

But that is for later, not for now.
      For now Nyokabi stands in front of this woman, this
woman who has the audacity to dismiss her grief. The only
woman in the world who might understand how she has moved
through me in the last few days. How the world has ended and
started over again and again in fragments.

"Wasted tears?"

Nyokabi touches her wet cheek and brings her finger to her
tongue. Salty.

"You," she says again, feeling the embers of the anger that
had been dissipating spark up again. This woman. Why? She
picks at the empty bottle in her skirt, realizes she did not ask the
question out loud. "Why?"

Ma Nyasi starts to speak but Kabi doesn't let her— she is
angry, so so angry, and now she has something to direct that
anger at. Thoughts coming out in fragments.

"I need to go back!"

          "I need more!"

                    "Tell me how to fix it."

Ma Nyasi looks at her sadly. "That is not the way it works,
Nyokabi."

"No!" She doesn't want to hear it. "I have to go back! I can
save him!" Baraka's words echo in the back of her mind. Her last
memory of him—*You don't get to always save me Kabi.*

"Did it change anything?" Ma Nyasi asks her now. She does
not step toward or away from Kabi—she looks like she is an
extension of the earth, rooted to the ground. "He is still dead, is
he not?"

This callousness with which Ma Nyasi speaks of death feeds

Kabi's anger. She throws the vial that her fingers have been caressing across the air, and it lands right next to Ma Nyasi's feet. "I can fix it!"

Ma Nyasi does not even flinch. "Kabi, you cannot fix anything. Going back only solidifies the way things will be. You haven't changed anything."

Kabi wants to hurt her the way she is hurting. "You're lying!" She points her finger at the woman, past the point of caring about respecting an elder. "The things they say about you are true! Mwendawazimu!"

And the woman laughs. Not a big laugh, or a happy one in any regard, but a small chuckle that carries weight. "I am just thinking of the…what is the word? Ahh, yes, the irony. You call me mad when you were the one shouting about your dead brother being alive."

Kabi spits on her. Ma Nyasi flinches. Her face hardens. She wipes saliva off her dress and straightens. "Foolish girl. It seems I have been wasting my time…and yours."

As she turns, Kabi panics. "Wait!" She does not know what she wants or needs to say, but she cannot let her go.

"Tell me why then!" She tries to be less angry. "Just," she falters., "What was the point then? Of all this? If I can't save him, *what was the point?*"

Ma Nyasi cocks her head and for once Kabi sees some feeling, not empathy or sympathy exactly, but something. Ma Nyasi sighs. "I thought it would help you heal."

Nyokabi is tired with this game. "Heal?!"

She closes her eyes and counts to ten times a hundred, refusing to let this woman win, refusing to let the madness in.

But she can hear Baraka calling her name.

"He was here." She opens her eyes. "Like you are here now. Real as the sun on my skin and the red soil beneath my feet. Every time I close my eyes I can smell him, the cocoa butter scent is so strong it overpowers everything else in this space, and I can hear his voice calling my name in different ways…

NYOKABI! when he is angry is not the same as

Kaaaabiiiii when he is excited about a new show he wants to show me, or the new nude foundation for dark skin," Kabi smiles as she says this. "Or a role he got in the Kenya National Theatre Production." The tears come back. She is learning that her body holds an endless supply of water.

Ma Nyasi grimaces.

"Wasted tears?" Kabi scoffs. "I can hear him! Do you understand that? That I could feel him? Touch his skin covered in goose bumps when he was cold?

The soft brown covering him,

                                        protecting his pulse,
                       still moving,
    his heart still beating.

How can I heal when your stupid potion made me believe that I could keep him alive?" Nyokabi is tired, has no new words left to add.

"You know this land will one day be yours?" Ma Nyasi gestures at the shamba they stand on.

Kabi bites her tongue to keep from snapping at the woman.

Ma Nyasi bends and picks up a handful of soil from the ground. "You mentioned how real the red soil is, and I just remembered how your mother and I used to play here when we were barely old enough to know our heads from our feet."

Kabi's mother does not like to bring up her family, has never talked about anything before her life in the city.

Ma Nyasi continues. "You see that house over there?"

The brick colonial-style structure over the fence barely looks qualified enough to be called a house. There is a wooden shack next door with smoke coming out of its makeshift chimney. Very different from her mother's inherited home, on this side of the fence, the side where Baraka is buried. *The one that used to be Guka's,* Nyokabi thinks.

She has only ever been to this shags thrice. The first time when Baraka was maybe three? Or four? She remembers Mama saying that Guka could not be left to live in this big house by himself, so she brought him to the city. There was no reason to come back until Guka died and they had his funeral here, but even then she was only eleven, too wrapped up in trying to keep

Baraka from making noise during the boring Kikuyu services to notice anything. Even then the responsible… oldest… daughter.

Then there is another time… another funeral? She cannot quite remember.

Ma Nyasi continues. "That one belonged to Cucu Ciru, your Maitu."

Kabi thinks Ma Nyasi must be confused. "I don't have a Maitu called Ciru. Do you mean Auntie Ciru? Mama's friend?"

Ma Nyasi looks at her sharply. "Assi! We! Be careful of refusing to claim your ancestors." She lets the soil she has been holding seep out through the spaces between her fingers and explains. "Ciru was your direct Maitu's younger sister, so she was your Maitu. She was also the last one to remain alive of my Maitu's children."

This is not the time to be given the family tree history, Kabi thinks, but Ma Nyasi will not be bothered with her thoughts.

"You know you are different, Kabi."

Nyokabi sighs. Her question has not been answered. "What do you mean?"

Ma Nyasi wipes her palms—stained brown now—on her skirt. "Well, you are a storyteller aren't you? Your mother once told me that you were pursuing a career as a writer."

Kabi rolls her eyes. Slaving away at a copy editing job while writing bad poetry in private does not necessarily equate to being a storyteller but she says none of this. Ma Nyasi wraps an arm around Kabi and nudges her towards the direction of the fence. "Aha, naweza kuambia hadithi?"

Kabi's frustration is bubbling up again. "I don't want another story! I just… I just want my brother back. I want to know how to bring Baraka back."

Ma Nyasi squeezes Kabi's shoulder once then walks towards the house, expecting her to follow. "I'll make us some tea."

For all the anger that still sits inside Kabi, a resignation comes in to share space with it. She needs answers at least. It's the least she can get.

The furnishings inside the house are sparse. Old black and white photos hang on the wall. Kabi cannot recognize anyone in them, *ancestors* she thinks, and wonders where they all are. *Is Baraka with them?* There on the right wall stands a glass bookshelf with odds and ends inside it. An old bright red sofa set has white doilies placed in a very particular—two and then three's—arrangement. The house is not beautiful by any standard but it is clean, lived in.

"At least it's not the grass."

Ma Nyasi who is in the kitchen now moving things around shouts, "Ati?"

"I thought you lived in the grass," Kabi says without thinking, then realizes what she has said.

Ma Nyasi is laughing. "My nickname precedes me."

She comes out with a flask in one hand and two tin mugs, ugly peach flowers drawn on the sides of them. She places them on the low glass table—also covered in doilies—which sits in the centre of the room. "I am sorry I do not live up to the myths that have been told about me."

Kabi looks at this 'mad' woman who does not show emotion and she thinks that she looks surprisingly normal—in her kitenge wraps—pouring two cups of tea, an almost smile on her face. Kabi is struck by this brief moment of the ordinary in the midst of, well, everything else in time.

Ma Nyasi carries a wooden sugar bowl and a little silver teaspoon mid-air hovering over the steaming cups on the table. "Sukari?"

Kabi responds instantly. "Dufia."

Ma Nyasi pauses, goes still for a few seconds and then says as she places two heaped spoons into her own cup. "My Sifa used to take her tea sugarless also." She takes a trial sip from her own mug, murmurs contentedly, then adds, "I always thought it was strange. An old woman's habit in a young woman's body."

That's right, Nyokabi thinks, *Ma Nyasi lost someone too.* "Did you go back?"

Ma Nyasi places the other steaming cup in Kabi's cold hands. It burns at first, her fingers taking a moment to adjust to the sudden temperature change.

After an extended silence, Kabi adds. "So you couldn't save

her then?" She does not wait for a response. "She's not here,
so you obviously couldn't save her." The weight of this truth
begins to sink in for Kabi, pushing out her denial, Baraka's voice
lingering. *You don't get to always save me Kabi.*

Ma Nyasi sucks on her teeth. "Iwe! Drink your tea.
Itapoesha."

When Kabi has taken a sip, Ma Nyasi speaks quietly. "No, I
did not bring her back." She pauses. "Not in the way you think."

Kabi looks at Ma Nyasi, who does not expound, and realizes
she is not fully here. *Ha*, she thinks, *not fully now?* She sips her tea,
quells her frustration.

"This thing that we have did not come with instructions Kabi.
The problem with us is that we always like to control things."
Ma Nyasi shakes her head. "Ayiii yawah! Human nature is really
a mystery, but not so much as time. You see even now you're
here saying, *let me go back, let me save him*, as if it is your choice.
Chi! We cannot dictate time, kairetu, even though…even though
some of us can carry it."

Kabi barely keeps her frustration in check. "Stop talking in
circles, woman!"

Breathe. She reminds herself to count one to ten times a
hundred. She should have realized by now that Ma Nyasi will
speak when she wants to speak about what she wants to speak
about only in her own time.

Ma Nyasi still looks unbothered by the little outburst. "Do
you know why they started calling me mwendawazimu? Or, as
you prefer, Ma Nyasi?"

Kabi knows the story her mother gave her, of a woman who
went to live in the grass and practiced witchcraft, to be a half
truth. She shakes her head.

"Well, my name is Njeri so maybe you can test that out on
your tongue instead of this Mad Ma Nyasi nonsense." She sips
her tea and continues. "Yes I went back, Kabi. I went back the
day they were burying Sifa, and I…"

The third time they visited! Kabi remembers a new fragment. She
must have been twelve or thirteen, not long after Guka's burial.
A woman thrashing on the ground.

"I told them not to bury her. I jumped into the hole they had dug...well at least I think so. Sikumbuki viillee lakini fragments I remember."

How had Kabi forgotten this memory? It was resurfacing vaguely. Baraka had stayed home with dad. Mum had said it was just a quick quick funeral for a relative. Kabi remembers staring at the crazy woman who jumped into the grave with the casket. It had taken three men to pull her out, screaming and thrashing.

On the way home, Mum refused to talk about it, telling Kabi she must have imagined such things, it was not all that. *Just forget about it*. And so she had.

Ma Nya—Njeri—places her palms on the sides of her head, massaging her temples. Her expression is far away still, lost somewhat, but detached. Not really *sad*. "What I remember, from when I went back, is my daughter's voice. That last morning we talked on the phone. All the different ways it happened. All the different times I went back, to make it happen differently. I carry all of those conversations in my head."

Ma Njeri shifts in her seat, remembers her tea, draws it up to her lips. "But now is not the time for that story. Now is the time for another one."

No, it cannot end there, Nyokabi thinks. Out loud, she asks, "What happened?"

"Nothing..." Njeri sighs. "Everything. It's just, just not the way it works, Kabi." Sips tea. "Tell me, when you went back did you feel anything? In your body?"

Now it is Kabi's turn to be quiet, but Njeri insists. "Look at me, Kabi. You felt it, didn't you? Ehh?"

Kabi does not want to talk about the headaches, the searing pain that felt like a thousand needles pricking her brain repeatedly. She does not want to contemplate what that might mean. "You said you have a story to tell me." She tries to get the woman back on track.

Ma Nyasi touches a key on a chain around her neck. "Cucu Ciru gave me this." Kabi is amazed by her ability to move from subject to subject as if they are all part of the same thought.

"Well, left it for me, I should say, after she died. It was her mother's—Maitu Njeri—who I was named for."

Fragments.

And this is how it goes.
Younger woman listening to older woman,
Little tin cups in their hands, the smell of tangawizi
warmth seeping out, disappearing with the time.
Story-traveling-between-now-and-then…
Ancestor who picked purple flowers, red roots,
and stinging nettles that were offered by the earth
to those who could carry me.

Nyokabi does not realize that she is sitting at the edge of her seat, hairs standing up on her skin. She could never resist a good story. "What happened?"

Ma Nyasi repeats the odd answer that means a thousand different things. "Nothing…Everything."

Kabi is coming to terms with the fragments of this circular-speaking, time-carrying woman. "Deja vu," she says, and remembers the last time she held these words was with Baraka.

Of lives lived and repeated.

Njeri does not hear her, or hears her but chooses to ignore her, answering her previous question instead. "According to my Cucu, Maitu Njeri got lost in time."

Nyokabi is not sure she heard correctly. "Lost in time?"

"The story goes that she travelled back too many times," Njeri says. "The time mix potion—kumbuka—it does not work on everyone, only particular people…mostly storytellers, poets, healers…those who already know that time does not move in a straight line. The ones that already have time carrying in them.

If they train hard enough, go back enough times, they can go back without Kumbuka and carry time more specifically instead of being dropped randomly any-when." She fingers the rim of her now empty mug

"Maitu Njeri was one of them. She became a practiced time carrier. First, it was just to bring back Meketilili."

Kabi raises an eyebrow. "Meketelili wa Medza? But—"

"But," Njeri interrupts, "As you and I have learned—time does not work like that. Maitu Njeri thought maybe if she could go back even further, back to Mepoho, back to Syokimau, she could make the people believe them. She would show them that she was from a Kenya that was already living the prophecies, and prepare them more for the coming of the white man."

Nyokabi encourages Njeri to continue. "And then?"

"Well, she always ended up in *this* version of history. You see, this time carrying was not new. Maitu learned from the women she lived through, the prophetesses who already knew. Syokimau knew her name would live after her but that would not change the way things would be. Aha! And see the railway that now passes through the land she walked. This long snake that hisses people from one place to the next. She knew."

. "What about Mepoho? Meketilili?" Nyokabi asks. "The other ones she went back to?"

Njeri smiles sadly. "There are two different versions of this story that Cucu Ciru gave me. On some days, she would say nothing her mother did changed anything that came after. On other days, she would say that one of the reasons that our Mjikenda warrior was able to walk 1,000 kilometers—when she escaped prison and exile to get back to her people—was because Maitu Njeri brought Meketilili food and led her to safe places to sleep, found her roots and leaves from the forest to heal her blisters and her wounds."

Kabi asks, "So you can change what happened?"

Njeri shakes her head. "The question you should be asking is who really saved who? Seeing the resilience of the prophetess firsthand changed Maitu irrevocably. When she returned to her time, Maitu Njeri spread the warrior stories of these women, reminding the workers to remember. *Aha!* she said. *Do not forget the healers and prophets! Do not fall for the white man's lying tongue!* But the work ravaged her body and her soul."

Njeri pauses. "Cucu told me that, in the later years, when Maitu Njeri would have conversations with the air. Talking to Mekatilili, Mepoho, Syokimau and others as if they had come back with her. Then one day she just left, and did not come back."

Ma Nyasi stands up abruptly. "More tea?"

Kabi does not really want to drink anything, but her tin cup is cold and she misses the warmth in her fingers. She gulps the rest of the cold milky liquid down and stretches out her mug.

"Tsi tsi. Lost in time. That's the way it works." Ma Nyasi clicks her tongue and hands the now full cup back to Kabi. "Not in a line—not in a way that we can predict— yes, we can carry time, but it also carries us."

She refills her own cup halfway, stops, then pours again, deliberately looking for that perfect three quarter's full stopping point. "What did it feel like?"

Kabi responds with a quizzical glance. Mama Kabi sits. "My question from the beginning...to your body. What did it feel like?"

Kabi remembers the nausea in the car ride, the dizziness, shaking, and feeling like nothing was steady, having to hold on to Baraka's arm for support at the mall, falling to the ground. The pounding head at the basketball court, blinding pain in the house, sliding to the ground.

Small small things, she thought. More important to be able to feel him, hear him, touch him, knowing he was still moving,
   breathing,

                    sweating,
            muscles contracting,

                              blood flowing,
                              heart beating.

Small, small things, she thinks, then says out loud, "It hurt." *But not as much as losing him,* she doesn't say.

Njeri nods knowingly. "I could not stop throwing up for days when I went back. Both in and out of time." She touches the

wrinkles on her own faded skin. "It is not easy on the body,
Kabi, this carrying of time. Every time you go back, you carry a
little bit of now into then and every time you return…" She rests
her head against the back of her chair, closes her eyes.

Not all here. Not all now.

"When I am closing my eyes…focus…just a little. Ahhh, there
she is. I carried bits and pieces of her back with me." She opens
her eyes. "You said you still hear him, yes?"

Nyokabi nods, not sure where this is going.

"Every time we return, we bring bits of then into now."
She shakes her head, as if trying to remove something from
her brain. "Yes, hard on the body this work is. Something so
small, so fragile, like the human consciousness is not meant to
transport—to carry—something so heavy, so *unstructured*."

She looks steadily at Kabi. "You cannot go back."

The words are slow to enter Kabi's awareness, crawling into
her senses, and settling in her skin. Njeri continues. "Maitu
Njeri… she went and she came and she went and she came until
her consciousness could not return. Until she was lost to all the
different times and people she had seen. I learned the hard way
Kabi. Trust."

Denial. "But," Kabi whispers, "I can save him."

"Listen to me, Kabi. You must let go."

This is not where she wanted this story to go. Kabi calls on her
anger, the only energy source she has left. "How can you just give
up like that? Knowing what we can do? Knowing what the the
Kumbuka gives us access to? How can you just let it go to waste?"

Kabi puts the mug down sloppily, tea spilling over the sides,
staining a small patch on the white doily. Some of the hot tea
pours onto the back of her hand burning her skin and suddenly
she sees Baraka burning his skin, briefly, vaguely; deja vu. "How
can I let go when I know he is still out there?

Still alive?

How?"

Njeri's eyes are drawn to the spreading stain, stopping just
where a flower begins, but she does not move. Does not stand up
to get a rag. "She lost a brother too."

"Huh?"

"Meketilili, I mean. Maybe it is not important." Ma Nyasi shrugs. "Maybe it is. But whatever the case, it is part of her story. They don't talk about it as much now, but she had a brother who was kidnapped and killed when she was just a child. All of these stories begin before the traveling, before the prophecies, before the time-carrying, back when it was just the storyteller and her love and her loss and her grief."

"You know, Kabi, the story I have told you—*am telling you*—is only one version of events, and as you know with all stories there are always different tellings, each carrying a little truth. The other version of this story, the one that everyone else believes, is the version where Maitu Njeri lost her mind."

"In the other version," Njeri continues, "the old woman, disillusioned by the state of her people, started claiming God-like powers. She was just like every mad person before her, speaking to air as if it could carry on conversation like people. In this version, the old woman invoked the names of the dead and addressed them as if they were still alive. Here she is not special, a storyteller, or a healer, or a prophetess. Here she is merely senile.

"In this version, her granddaughter, my mother, inherits her madness and marries a man who thinks that marrying a woman, any woman—even if she is called schizophrenic by muzungu doctors—will prove to the world and to himself that he is man enough.

"In this version their daughter, Maitu Njeri's great granddaughter, rightly named after her, is just another mad woman waiting to happen; mwendawazimu—mad ma Nyasi— all the names she will grow into.

"In this version, the little Njeri listens to her Cucu Ciru's stories that romanticize the madness which took both her mother and her daughter from her.

"In this version, the girl's Cucu teaches her how to keep it hidden, this madness, until one day, after all the women before her, are gone, the one name that keeps Njeri grounded and rooted to the earth's idea of sanity is taken from her.

"And now we have loss-death-grief finally breaking this

woman's resistance to madness."

Njeri fiddles with the key on the chain around her neck, stands up, and walks to the shelf in the corner of the room. She removes a box from the corner. She places the box on the table. "This is where it all started."

Nyokabi meets her eyes over the box.

"I resigned myself to the label of madness that I have inherited. That day of Sifa's burial…I remember fragments. I remember pulling at my hair until it came away from the roots. I remember asking to be buried with her, saying, *why not just kill me too if you are so intent on murder*? That day they remembered I was the daughter of the naked woman who was found drowned, face down in the dam. The word they could not remember properly, until someone…Daktari maybe? Someone from the city voiced the thing they were trying to remember. *Schizophrenia*. And they all remembered. That day my madness was not pardoned by my grief." She laughs a sad laugh.

"Baba Sifa had done the thing that was expected of the man whose woman cannot control herself properly. *To take care of her.* He tried to check me into Mathare. Of course, he didn't follow up. It was just so that he could look like he had done something." Njeri gives Nyokabi a curious look. "Noni is the one that signed me out."

Kabi is taken aback. "Noni who?"

Njeri clicks. "Don't be so surprised. Your mother. She is more than just the version of herself that you have experienced, Kabi."

Nyokabi turns away. It's like Ma Nyasi can see right through her, calling out her resentment.

Njeri continues with a knowing smile. "And besides, we women know what it is like to not be believed, ehh? We are called mad so that it is easier to dismiss what we have to say. Hurrmph. Especially in our family. Your mother resists it.

"But me? Ehh me, I just said to hell with it! Let them call me what they want. Let them decide I am not right in the head. As long as I could get Sifa back.

"As long as I could carry her—the version of her that was— into the space where she wasn't."

Ma Sifa—Njeri—holds her left breast. To Kabi, she looks like she is in pain but then she continues. "Me, I have resigned myself to all the different versions of the story, kairetu. Madness is lonely but I have made my peace. But you, you are still young. Too young, mpenzi. Death has visited you too early and…and of the most tragic kind."

Kabi hates that everyone has skirted around this word, referring to it without saying it. "Suicide," she says with closed teeth. "Just say it!"

Njeri nods her head, measures her words. "Past choices, Kabi. Choices that were not yours, choices that you cannot carry. But the choices for now…"

She drifts off, looks up at the ceiling as if the correct words are written somewhere up there. She narrows her eyes, trying to find them."The choices for now must take into consideration that your family still needs you. That your parents cannot afford to lose two children."

Responsible

Oldest

Daughter.

Kabi is tired of this expectation.

"Whichever version of this story is the correct one Kabi, whichever version is true—" Ma Nyasi looks back down, one hand playing with the key on the chain around her neck, the other fiddling with the front of the wooden box in front of her. " —both versions lead you to the same destination. Whether lost in time or lost in madness, you will always end up lost."

"Then why?"

Ma Nyasi stops fiddling with the front of the box but she does not look up at Kabi. "You said you can hear him still, can smell him, feel his skin, if you close your eyes? I was not lying when I said healing, kairetu. You carried parts of him back with you, parts that are still alive to you now, and you are a storyteller, so you can articulate those parts of him for those who might forget. That is healing."

Kabi's shoulders slump. It does not feel like healing. She looks down at her cup of tea, tears brimming.

Ma Nyasi continues, "Or maybe I am just an old selfish woman tired of carrying time by myself. Asiii! Maybe I just wanted someone else to see the world the way that I do. It is lonely to be the only one that knows how time really moves, not one way, but zigzag, and still I am powerless to make the world anything other than what it is.

Ha! Asssiiiweee!"

Kabi focuses on the hot mug in front of her. There is too much moving from one side of her body to the other. She zones out briefly.

"... other people you know?"

Ma Nyasi's words intercept Kabi's absentmindedness. "Huh?"

"The other people I gave the potion? The ones before you? For most of them it just put them in a deep sleep."

Kabi nods, not fully registering the words.

Njeri says in a final tone. "Not everyone can carry time, Kabi. Kumbuka Kumbukumbu."

What to say? What to ask?

Kabi thinks. Phone vibrates as she reaches for it. Just now notices: *7 missed calls.*

Weh' knowing her mother if all the missed calls are hers, this would be it for Kabi. *I might be joining you sooner than anticipated Baraka,* she thinks, barely smiles. Dark humour. He would have hated it.

Ma Nyasi looks at the clock. "Hya! It is getting late!" She stands up and gives Kabi a cheeky look. "We must have gotten lost in time." She winks. Kabi rolls her eyes. The woman clears the cups from the table, leaves the flask and the box mumbling about sorting that out later.

"Acha niende choo haraka alafu nikupeleke kwa watu wako."

Kabi mmhmm's in agreement and then hears her phone beep. From an hour ago. Her phone must be bugging. She opens it.

Baba:

I have taken mum home. She was not great.

Mentioned you were with her cousin.

Call your aunty ciru. Will give you lift home.

Another from just five minutes ago:

TATA CIRU

Hya!

Kairetu your father told me you were talking with one of the other aunties.

Wea? Tried to call but the phone was not going thru. Are u ok? Just concerned. I was overseeing the tent take down & the catering people. Heh it's hard to find good help anywhere these days. Nyway. I'm by the parking in front of the big house. Ready to go whenever u r.

But it's getting late, kama tunaweza harikisha kidogo it'll be good!

KABI
Ok see you at home!

Kabi sends her father. And to the other:

KABI
coming! will be there in 5!

Ma Nyasi is in the bathroom now. Kabi shouts. "It's okay, Ma... err.. Njeri! Tata Ciru is waiting for me so I'll just leave now!"

"Are you sure?" Njeri calls out, but she does not sound disappointed.

Kabi starts walking towards the door, then turns without really thinking about it, picking up the little obscure wooden box from the glass table. "Mmhmm. Yes!" she calls back.

Is it possible for a thing to feel both heavy and light at the same time?

"Thank you for the tea!" Kabi stops herself from running out the door, keeping a steady pace until she is at the flimsy fence that separates the two sides of the same land.

When she is on the other side, she runs to where most of the cars were parked. And there is Tata Ciru in her colourful kitenge outfit. Trust her to wear only colour to a funeral—colours more muted, to be fair, than her usual yellows and pinks and oranges but the dark red and soft brown still stands out. They would make her very easy to spot in a crowd, not that there is any crowd now.

The two men her aunty is talking to both turn to the two trucks that are already half full with folded tents. Tata Ciru sees her running towards them and smiles wildly.

"Hya! We were about to call a search party!" She notices Kabi's frantic look. "Are you okay?"

Kabi nods, catching her breath. She looks around for the infamous yellow Volkswagen that Tata Ciru has had longer than it should probably be legal to have a car. She tries to make her voice sound normal. "Can we goJust a little out of breath."

Tata doesn't look convinced, but she opens up the car. "Sure thing, sweetie."

She turns to the men with boxes and the pickup trucks. "Hya asanteni! Tutaongea kesho."

One nods his head in affirmation and the other gives a thumbs up.

She slides into the driver's seat, buckles in and starts the engine. And off... they... go...

In fragments

Left behind, in a house that stands on ground that carries histories in its graves, a woman talks to a daughter who is not really there, arguing about me. If seen through the window, some would say she is talking to the air.

"She took it!" This woman, who goes by many names, says out loud, fingering the key to the chain around her neck. She is afraid for the girl but does not say this part out loud.

Was it locked?

She thinks but does not want to answer, does not want to know the answer. "I told her not to take it. I warned her, I did."

She closes her eyes and before her are all the women whose stories she has travelled through, carrying bits of all of them back with her. But she looks for one. *Focus*. One in particular. *There.*

Sifa's smile

Sifa's little round nose

Sifa's eyes

Sifa's big pink lips

Sifa's long chin

Sifa's voice… Voice?

She can hear her a thousand different ways.

The mad woman, the little girl Njeri, the grass mother, all open their eyes and she lifts her arms around to the back of her neck, unlocking the chain that has sat there for decades, and she tosses it outside the open window as far as she can.

"Good riddance!"

Njeri walks back to the kitchen, placing some water in a sufuria, adds half a cup of milk, two tablespoons of majani—she cannot stand weak tea—turns on the jiko, cuts up fresh ginger as the nylon starts to simmer.Time dreamer, time speaker, time carrier. She throws finely cut ginger into the now browning mixture and inhales it. *A watched pot never boils,* she remembers one of Cucu's sayings. You cannot make anything happen quicker or slower than it wants to.

Haraka haraka,
Haina Baraka

A blessing, this boy that she never even knew, bringing her life full circle. *His sister…hmm?*

The tea is overflowing. She switches off the jiko, takes a clean tin mug off the dishrack, and sieves the steaming liquid into it, letting the aroma fill her nostrils.

Two sugars.

Time has never been able to take away her sweet tooth. She says out loud. "A young woman's habit in an old woman's body." She walks back to the ugly red sofa set and sits. A sip. Boiling hot. "Perfect," she whispers. *Good riddance,* she thinks.

She closes her eyes. Calling the past into now, all the women she travelled through by inheritance. All the pasts she has carried in fragments.

One name she calls out.

"Sifa?"

There she is…but when is she?

NYOKABI
STORYTELLER
TIME-CARRIER

I wake up and the moon is out; a half moon. I yawn and stretch, feel my hands cramp. I rub the back of my neck and think of Baraka then baba.

"Wakey wakey sleeping beauty!"

Tata Ciru is still on the driver's wheel, looking perky as ever. "You fell asleep," she says. I look at my phone—it's going to midnight.

"How far are we?" My groggy voice sounds far removed from me.

"Not veeerrrryyyyy," she says. This could mean anything from 10 to 100 kilometers.

I sigh.

"Usijali. Tutafika tu."

Tata Ciru looks so awake that I believe her. *How does she always have so much energy?*

"What's in the box?" she points in the direction of the stolen thing that I have been holding onto all through my unintentional sleep. I didn't think I would actually get away with it., I probably still won't.

Phones exist. Ma Nyasi—*Njeri*, I correct myself— will probably call immediately I get to Nairobi, if she hasn't already called Mama and told her about it. Damn.

"Nothing," I answer...too quickly? Wait a heartbeat, then

add, "Everything." Softer.

Tata Ciru's lips part slightly, into her almost always about-to-say-something expression, but she changes her mind about whatever it is that she wanted to say, remains quiet for all of thirty seconds, then asks, "Want to drive?"

I suspect she is trying to fill the space with words, trying to avoid saying— asking—the dreaded *Have you stopped believing your dead brother is still alive?*

I shake my head, let her stew in the silence I know makes her uncomfortable.

"Hey?" she looks at me tentatively.

"Yeah?" I respond, barely.

"I have this friend…"

My fingers, needing something to do, trace the outline of the box.

"Well, she's a good friend of mine, Kabi, a really good friend. You know? Those ones you don't want to take for granted? Well anyway, her name is Annie and she is a therapist. But not one of those shoddy ones who don't know what they're doing." She moves one of her hands from the wheel and waves it in the air to emphasize her point. Tata Ciru is the type of person who cannot talk without her hands. I watch them instead of listening.

"…very good recommendations. Very good! So I was thinking, well maybe, I was thinking I could pay for a few sessions for you to go?"

I remain silent. She looks at me quickly then turns her gaze back to the road, right hand returned onto the steering wheel. "Just a few sessions, I was thinking. You know? You can just try it out. See if you like it, and if you don't…it's fine still."

I wonder if she had this conversation with my parents? Did they ask her to get their mad daughter some help? I am beginning to realize that soft anger has become a constant state of being. Almost always half there, waiting to be called upon…I count one to ten times a hundred.

Breathe, I think, but say nothing.

Five minutes pass, then ten. The longest silence we've had since I have been awake. After thirty minutes have passed, I still do not know anything about where we are, except that the half-moon has been hidden by the clouds.

Tata Ciru says, "We all miss him, Kabi. You know?"

Maybe it is the way she says-asks it. Tata, whose presence I have always taken for granted, surprises me every once in a while. She is so different from Mum, always colourful and always ready to do this and that for no other reason than it is something that can be done.

Tata Ciru who bought Baraka his first Dera when he was fourteen and convinced Mum to let him keep it. Tata Ciru who got irritated very quickly but also got over her irritation even more quickly while Mum was one to sit in her righteous anger until she was convinced the person who did her wrong reaped what they sowed. How the two of them became best friends still baffles me.

I can hear Baraka telling me to be softer. *She loved you. I know.*

What right have I to own grief?

I think of Njeri's statement.

The wood of the box in my lap is so smooth. Ma Nyasi's words come back to me. *Madness is lonely.* I make a decision.

I turn to Tata Ciru and say, "Tell me about your friend Annie."

She smiles, removes her right hand from the wheel and squeezes my shoulder briefly, then delves into a monologue, excitedly talking about the success rates Annie has had. She was even interviewed on NTV the other day, she tells me.

Hya, maybe Mama and Baba could see her also? Yes, actually, now that she thinks about it, it would be a wonderful idea if they were all able to go for family counselling. "I know it would do Noni a world of good!"

Tata Ciru wonders out loud if it would be a conflict of interest since she is her friend. She goes on and on, only needing the occasional nod of the head and *mmhmm* as encouragement from me, to continue.

My thoughts wander back to the last long short car ride I took. Baraka's hands on the wheel.

Kumbuka Kumbokumbo.

Still tracing the outline of the box, I suddenly remember the key on the chain around Njeri's neck. "Stupid," I whisper to myself.

Tata Ciru stops mid-sentence. "Did you say something?"

I shake my head. "No. I'm listening."

She goes on and I want to laugh at myself, or cry. I didn't really think that one through, did I? But it's fine. I have already made my decision, haven't I? *Your parents need you,* Ma Nyasi had said. Kenneth and Noni Kimani, still here, still part of my world, and me their

Responsible

Oldest

Daughter.

Who I am. Who I always will be. *Leave the past in the past,* I think. I will do the right thing. I should really pay more attention to Tata.

My fingers fidget with the front of the box. *Just as well,* I think, pulling at the lid absentmindedly.

Slight resistance.

Open space.

I gasp—"Shit!"—and draw back my stung finger.

"What's wrong?" Tata Ciru asks, graciously not commenting on the explicative I just uttered.

"Nothing!" I say… *Everything,* I think. Too many feelings run through my senses, and I'm overwhelmed by the sweet, savoury, sour, honey, pungent, thick, bitter, soft everything-scent that comes with time.

It is difficult to explain what to do with the juxtaposition of coming to terms with what one cannot control and being brought into a world of possibilities, understanding that the only constant thing in life is change.

And maybe it is still possible.

The box is open.

Time is open.

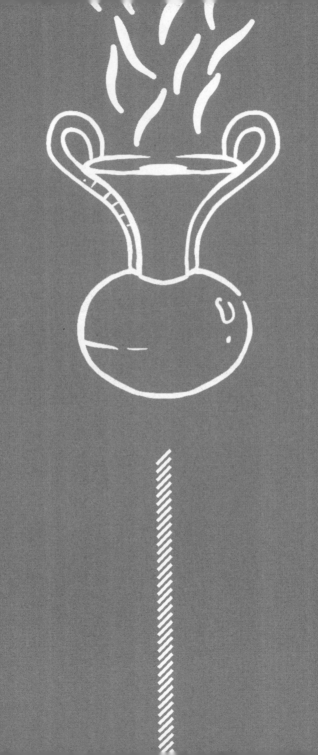

THE END

ACKNOWLEDGMENTS

Whenever I teach, I tell my students that neither stories nor any form of art exists in a vacuum. All of what I create is possible because of those who have created before me and those who I get to experience creating around me.

I am so grateful for all the storytellers in my life.

Specifically shouting out the books that gave me permission, as I was writing this novella.

Augustown by Kei Miller will forever be a source of permission to believe the versions of the story that have not had the luxury of being written down (ironic i know).

Kamau Brathwaite for permission to write the way my people speak, to think about the project of decolonizing language, and to pay attention to how Englishes work in different spaces.

The Deep by Rivers Solomon permitted me to think of the burden of the storyteller as a carrier of history and how, as much as remembering the past may give, when it is a solo endeavour, it also takes away.

To the first readers of and believers in this story: Valo, Mshai, Jenny, and Mnesh.

My MFA workshop class for sitting through the first drafts, and my professors: Karan Mahajan and Laird Hunt.

Voodoonauts community (Yvette, H.D, and L.P. especially) for supporting, loving, and adding to this work.

NAIWA, for being the most wonderful Kenyan writers support group.

Clarion Ghost Class, for becoming writing fam. <3

Arley, who first allowed for Baraka's story to be given to the world.

dave! Best publisher ever!

The Women ancestors that fought for our freedoms but were not written into the history books. Thank you for allowing me to remember you in these ways.

Kenyan Queer Community. For resisting and loving and finding ways to stay alive in a state that does not fight for your life. <3

Holy Spirit. Ruach. Pepo. Life Source. For guiding, teaching, healing, and navigating with me through my own grief.

About the Author

Shingai Njeri Kagunda is an Afrofuturist freedom dreamer, Swahili sea lover, and Femme Storyteller among other things, hailing from Nairobi, Kenya. She is currently pursuing a Literary Arts MFA at Brown University. Shingai's short story "Holding Onto Water" was longlisted for the Nommo Awards 2020 & her flash fiction "Remember Tomorrow in Seasons" was shortlisted for the Fractured Lit Prize 2020. She has been selected as a candidate for the Clarion UCSD Class of 2020/2021. #clarionghostclass. She is also the co-founder of Voodoonauts: an afrofuturist workshop for black writers.

About the Press

Neon Hemlock is a Washington, DC-based small press publishing speculative fiction, rad zines, and queer chapbooks. We punctuate our titles with oracle decks, occult ephemera, and literary candles.

Learn more about us at www.neonhemlock.com and on Twitter at @neonhemlock.